# MAN to MAN

Published by Phaze Books
Also by G.A. Hauser

Miller's Tale

Teacher's Pet

Pirates

Vampire Nights

# MAN to MAN

G.A. Hauser

*Phaze*
EXCEPTIONAL EROTIC FICTION

Man to Man Copyright © 2010 by G.A. Hauser

All rights reserved under the International and Pan-American Copyright Conventions. No part of this book may be reproduced or transmitted in any form or by any means, electronic or mechanical including photocopying, recording, or by any information storage and retrieval system, without permission in writing from the publisher.

The scanning, uploading and distribution of this book via the Internet or via any other means without the permission of the publisher is illegal, and punishable by law. Please purchase only authorized electronic editions, and do not participate in or encourage the electronic piracy of copyrighted materials. Your support of the author's rights is appreciated.

Warning: The unauthorized reproduction or distribution of this copyrighted work is illegal. Criminal copyright infringement, including infringement without monetary gain, is investigated by the FBI and is punishable by up to 5 years in federal prison and a fine of $250,000.

This is a work of fiction. Names, characters, places and incidents either are the product of the author's imagination or are used fictitiously, and any resemblance to any actual persons, living or dead, events, or locales is entirely coincidental.

A Phaze Books Production
Phaze Books
an imprint of Mundania Press LLC
6470A Glenway Avenue, #109
Cincinnati, Ohio 45211-5222

To order additional copies of this book, contact:
books@mundania.com
www.mundania.com

Cover Art © 2010 by SkyeWolf
SkyeWolf Images (http://www.skyewolfimages.com)
Edited by Stephanie Balistreri

Trade Paperback ISBN: 978-1-60659-499-5

First Edition • July 2010

Production by Mundania Press LLC
Printed in the United States of America

10  9  8  7  6  5  4  3  2  1

# Prologue

The water was black from the dark clouds above. Waves slapped the shore like God's hand punishing the earth. Tanner Cameron's heart was pumping in his throat. The LA County rescue boat could do nothing to help him as the one-man crew struggled to keep his craft from slamming into the coast.

With the rescue buoy trapped between himself and the victim, Tanner swam for shore. Over the roar of the water, he heard the whelping, high pitch of the medic's siren in the distance. Finding his feet on the sand, he dragged the unconscious man out of the raging sea to dry land. He dropped to his knees and began CPR. *Come on. Come on. Breathe!* Puffing air into the young man's mouth, Tanner's compressions jarred the man's chest to force him to come back to life. He returned to the man's mouth once more, pressing their lips together. He was so young. Twenty? *Breathe!*

When the fire crew arrived, Tanner was all too glad to give the young man over. He was exhausted. Sitting back on his heels, he watched the medics continue CPR as they loaded the man onto the rescue rig. As the truck barreled over the soft sand, Tanner caught his breath, touching his lips lightly.

The kiss of life.

It always felt personal to him.

Lowering his head, he tried to get his emotions under control. This was his job. Saving people. He only wished he had time to save himself.

# Chapter One

His lungs were aching. Josh Elliot leaned over, hands on knees, gasping for air. Salt water ran down his skin and his body felt numb from the exertion.

"Well done."

Barely acknowledging the pat on the back, Josh forced himself to stand straight and place one foot in front of the other on the wet sand. All that mattered was he'd done it. Finished in the top eighty so he could qualify. *No, I finished in the top fucking five! Holy Christ.*

"You all right?"

Another hand touched the small of his back. Josh looked up at one of the permanents, the lifeguards who held full-time positions. With his chest still expanding with the compelling need for air, Josh felt his breath catch in his throat.

Sky blue eyes reflecting the sunlight and seawater, over six foot in height with short cropped, dark brown hair, this man was a fucking god.

"Yeah. I'm all right." Josh licked the salt water off his top lip.

"That was an amazing time. Impressive."

"Was it?" Josh lit up as the man's broad smile glowed, set off by his golden skin.

"Yes. You should be proud of yourself. What's your name?"

"Josh. Josh Elliot." He held out his hand.

"Nice to meet you, Josh. I'm Tanner Cameron. You're through the toughest part. The next step is the classroom training. I wouldn't worry. You'll do fine."

"Thanks." Josh released Tanner's hand slowly, allowing his gaze to wander down Tanner's broad chest and six-pack abs. Tanner wore the "medal of honor" as far as Josh was concerned. Red swimming trunks. A genuine lifeguard.

"Are you going to be full time?"

"I want to. I'm taking some time off from my job and I'd like to not have to go back."

"Your *real* job?" Tanner smiled knowingly.

"Yes." Josh had fully recuperated from the thousand meter swim and felt his breathing ease.

Another man caught Tanner's attention. He nodded in acknowledgment. "I have to go. Great job, Josh. I hope to meet up with you again very soon."

"Me too." Josh watched as he walked down the crowded beach, admiring his strut and tight ass. "Holy shit. I wouldn't mind a piece of that." Someone shouting, gathering them together for instructions on getting their certificates and beginning the academy shook him out of his dreams.

※

Finally home, Josh dragged himself to the shower as the day's events caught up to him. Dropping his paperwork on the kitchen table of his four-room apartment, he stripped off his shorts and bathing suit and stood outside the shower door, waiting for the temperature to heat up. Looking back at the mirror, he noticed his shoulders were slightly singed even though he had coated himself with sunscreen. His ass was pure white compared to his darkly tanned back and legs. Stepping into the spray, Josh moaned with relief at washing the saline off his body, and the sand that seemed to get everywhere, including his ass crack and balls. Shampooing his hair, scrubbing his skin with a loofa, Josh floated over the day's events and the prospect of holding a lifeguard job over the summer. It was hard work. Not only was the physical training demanding but also the first aid American Red Cross certification, CPR, rescue techniques, the works.

He was ready. More than ready. After a four-year degree in business administration, he felt stuck in a lousy desk job.

He needed a change.

Josh shut off the taps, allowing the water to drip off his body, his head drooping with his weariness. He smoothed his hands down his chest and abs to swipe the water away. He brushed over his pubic hair and soft cock, considering jacking off. He couldn't. He was exhausted.

Wiping his face with a towel, he stepped out and continued to dry off catching his green eyes in the mirror's reflection.

"I don't know why you won't give me another chance."
"Because you went out on me behind my back, Luis."
"It didn't mean anything."
"It did to me."
"Josh, don't do this."
"Forget it, Luis. Forget it."
"But where will I find another man with eyes that green?"

Josh threw his towel over the shower door, leaned his palms on the sink, and stared at himself critically. Ending a six-month relationship sucked. No one was in his bed at the moment. Maybe it was another reason he had made the change in careers. He needed to get away from Luis. Seeing the man every day at work was killing him.

Josh heard his phone ringing and opened the bathroom door, hurrying to grab it. Standing naked in his kitchen, glimpsing the window with its partial view of the San Gabriel Mountains beyond the buildings across the street, Josh covered his groin in modesty as if a peeping tom in the apartment house opposite would be using binoculars.

"Hello?"
"Josh."
"What, Luis?"

"We need to talk."

"We do not need to talk." Josh was too tired to argue again.

"It was one time. One."

"What do you want from me? I just got back from the tryouts and I'm wiped." Josh scratched his balls gently.

"Oh. How did that go?"

"Fine." Josh wanted to hang up.

"I miss seeing you in the office."

"Come on, Luis, why are we going over and over old ground? I just stepped out of the shower and I need to eat something."

"Are you naked?"

Josh tugged on his soft cock and moved away from the window. "You need to stop calling me."

"I can't."

"You can. Believe me, you can." Josh opened the refrigerator for something to eat.

"Why won't you forgive me?"

"It wasn't working out anyway, Luis." Josh removed a bottle of water from the shelf and used his teeth to open the top, swigging it down. "Which is probably why you went out on me in the first place."

"That's not true."

"It is true." Josh wiped his mouth with the back of his arm. "Let me go. I really have to eat and lay down."

"I know once you become a lifeguard you'll have so many hard bodies to choose from I'll never cross your mind."

"That's the idea." Josh pictured Tanner instantly.

"Oh, screw you."

Smiling, Josh replied, "Now, that's the Luis I know and used to love. Goodbye, Luis." Josh disconnected the line, stuck the phone back in its cradle, and sucked down more water. Peering back at the window, he placed the water bottle on the counter and headed to his bedroom to put on a pair of shorts. Once he did, he sat on the bed in exhaustion and rubbed his face. Even though he was hungry, he dropped back on the spread, closed his eyes, and fell asleep.

# Chapter Two

Tanner stood on the lifeguard tower, binoculars to his eyes, his sunglasses propped on top of his head. The manic summer season had arrived with the anticipated flood of nearly sixty million visitors to California's thirty-one mile stretch of sandy beaches. It always brought him some anxiety. Tourists and regulars alike kept them busy. Too busy. Tanner was very glad the new recruits were being trained. The county needed them.

Tanner scanned the few surfers and bathers present during midweek, lowered the binoculars and dropped his sunglasses down on his nose.

"Hey."

Tanner waited as Destiny, another permanent, walked up the ramp to the tower in her red one-piece.

"Hi." Tanner stepped aside as she drew near.

"There's a cool breeze." She unfastened her hair from its clip, stuck the barrette between her teeth, twisting the blonde ponytail up in a knot behind her head again.

"Yes, it's perfect weather. I know it won't last."

Once she had fixed her hair, she leaned on the rail near him. "So, uh, Tanner…you feel like going out for a drink tonight?"

Though he knew he should socialize again sooner or later, the divorce had left him slightly lukewarm to the idea. And besides, Destiny was only twenty-two. As far as Tanner was concerned, eight years was more like fifty judging from Destiny's mental capacity.

"Uh…" He struggled to find a way to make the rejection sound kind and not nasty.

She moved toward him, brushing his arm lightly with hers. "Hm? One drink? After work?"

Tanner decided honesty was the best way to handle it. "Look, Destiny, I'm flattered. Really. But I'm still getting over a rough divorce and I'm not feeling ready for anything at the moment."

Pausing as if she were assessing the last sentence, she stared up at him and pouted like a child. "Not even for sex?"

*Yes, sex would be nice. No kidding. But sex with you would complicate my life, not simplify it.* Clearing his throat at the awkwardness, not to mention forwardness of her comment, Tanner muttered as he escaped, "I'm going to do some sprints while it's relatively quiet."

Quickly jogging down the ramp from the tower, Tanner fell into a comfortable pace as he ran on the wet sand.

He needed to get laid. No kidding. Months of court battles and bad blood, avoiding dating like the plague to not get trapped in yet another terrible rebound-type relationship, Tanner imagined hiring a hooker just to get his rocks off. He was sick of jacking off.

But Destiny was not his type. Though most of the women he worked with were beautiful, fit, and assertive, Tanner was slightly afraid to date one. He knew the gossip network would soon broadcast the information and he didn't want any animosity from his peers if the affair turned ugly. Besides, she was too young. A woman like Destiny, or Angelina and Samantha for that matter, were all young and vital. They wanted marriage and babies. Two things that Tanner did not want.

The child matter was what broke up his marriage. He did not want kids. Anna knew that the day she married him. Obviously, persistence held no time limit because five years later she assumed she could change his mind. She couldn't.

Turning back from where he'd come, Tanner jogged along his own footprints in the wet sand. Though it wasn't even eighty degrees, he was hot from the exercise and yearned for the breeze to cool him off.

So the battle began at home. Anna kept trying to make love without condoms. Tanner was certain she would cheat and get knocked up just to satisfy her motherhood instinct and he would be saddled with someone else's offspring. He stopped having sex with her just so he could be sure.

That made one year without.

One long-mother-fucking-year without getting laid. He was going insane.

Halting even with the tower, yet near to the water, Tanner dropped to the ground to start doing pushups. The sweat rolling off his nose and dripping onto the sand below him, he pumped as many as he could before he felt spent.

Sitting back on his heels, brushing the sand off his hands, he took a long look over the occupants of the water and beach, making sure he kept aware of everything around him even while he worked out.

He felt Destiny's eyes on him and hoped this was the end to her advances. The last thing he needed was to get a reputation as a jerk.

# Chapter Three

Five consecutive weekends, one hundred hours of training, grueling workouts, and cramming for tests, Josh felt as if he were back in college, but worse. The condensed version of the course and working with the fire department was intense. Fifty people, mostly men, made up the group of students all dying to finish the requirements and get the hell out onto the beach.

Wearing his navy blue academy t-shirt, kneeling, taking his test on a CPR dummy, Josh kept reminding himself of the alternative: getting back to that stuffy office, sitting in rush hour traffic, and feeling like a caged rat.

Every night that week, Luis had phoned. Josh stopped picking up, letting him whine into the answering machine while he studied his emergency medical technician assignments. He had enough on his plate. The last thing he needed was Luis clinging on for dear life. Maybe Josh needed a break from dating.

He'd had a boy-"friend" in high school who took his virginity, a bi-curious roommate to toy with in college, and he met Luis at work soon after he was hired. None of the three relationships were what he would call reciprocal or inspiring.

Maybe he needed to be alone for a little while. The yearning for a steady relationship with someone who loved him was wearing on him. He envied gay men who could screw around without getting attached. He'd never been one of those but, recently, he could see the benefits. The biggest problem Josh had was giving his heart too quickly. That and his terrible choices in men. He consistently opted for Mr. Wrong.

Trying not to lose track of his compressions and a little grossed out by kissing a piece of plastic, Josh sat back, placing his hand on the dummy's neck. The instructor shouted, "Pulse."

Josh relaxed. That was what he was hoping to hear. The subject had a pulse and was revived. Test over.

"That's fine, Josh."

Acknowledging the instructor, he stood, walked to the outer ring of students, and watched the next candidate get in position for the test.

The Manhattan Beach classroom was cool and comfortable. Josh gazed out of a window at the perfect blue sky, craving to be out in it. He'd had enough of four walls.

*≈*

Josh felt someone brush by his arm while he packed up his books.

"Hey, Josh."

"Emily." He smiled shyly.

"Pretty soon we'll be in our little red bathing suits."

"I can't wait. I'm ready." He filled his leather book bag and hung it on his shoulder.

"Want to go out for a quick bite?" She touched his arm again.

Having fended off women his whole life, Josh wondered what the appropriate time was to announce your preference. His classmates could very well end up on the same stretch of beach as he was. He wanted to gauge the attitude of his crew before he let that cat out of the bag. But he was out. He had no qualms about telling people if the opportunity arose.

"I'm really beat. I figured I'd just go home."

The disappointment on her pleasant face was palpable. Usually the women he'd confessed to either made a veiled, degrading comment, or the classic, "Why are all the pretty ones gay?" If he were honest with himself, he didn't need to hear either at the moment.

"That's a shame. I have to admit, Josh, I have a crush on you."

"That's very sweet." *Here we go.*

"Do you have a girlfriend?"

Taking a moment to assess who was within hearing distance, Josh suddenly got cold feet.

Men. The room filled with macho firemen and muscular lifeguards in training daunted him. Did he really need the sneers of disgust and whispers behind his back?

"No. But I'm really not in the market right now, Emily. I feel overwhelmed with my studies and just want to finish the course."

"I hear ya." She laughed it off politely. Her lashes dipped seductively as she lowered her voice to a purr, "If you ever change your mind, I'm available."

Josh knew any straight red-blooded male would hop on her in a heartbeat, he assumed it would seem somewhat unorthodox for him to pass. But he did. She didn't do a thing for him. She had breasts and no dick. It was the wrong combination to set him on fire.

"I'll keep that in mind." He smiled at her, waving as he slipped outside.

Josh set his book bag behind the driver's seat of his red Chrysler Sebring convertible and climbed in, enjoying the fantastic summer weather. He opened his glove compartment for his Ray-Bans and placed his sunglasses on his nose before he backed out of the space and headed home.

Cruising, the breeze blowing back his hair, Josh could not wait to get his first shift on the beach. Summer was here. How he loved summer.

❦

Josh came through the door, dumped off his books and hunted for food. The cupboards were bare so he called his favorite delivery service for a pizza. He dropped heavily on the sofa to study as he waited, kicking off his shoes and yanking his books out of his bag. Josh scratched out notes, highlighting lines.

The buzzer sounded an hour later. He jumped up, took his wallet out of his pocket and raced down the stairwell.

A young man stood outside with a cardboard pizza box. "Hey." Josh unlocked the lobby door and propped it open with his back.

"Fifteen dollars and sixty-three cents, man."

Josh found a twenty and exchanged the bill for the box, taking a closer look at the youth. Typical surfer dude, earring, pierced eyebrow, blond with blue eyes, Josh had a quick fantasy of inviting him up for more than a slice of pie. Christ, he was horny. There was something about the challenge and risk of seducing a straight man that lit his fire.

Imagining grabbing the guy's crotch for a squeeze, Josh shifted his weight as his dick became semi-erect.

"Here, dude."

Josh balanced the box and handed the boy back three of the singles. "For you."

"Thanks, man."

Josh watched him walk down the pathway back to his car with the plastic blue and red sign on it, licking his lips solemnly at the missed opportunity. His stomach grumbled from the aroma of the pizza.

Ascending the stairs barefoot, back to his unit, Josh nudged open the door and placed the pizza down on the counter. A plate, a napkin, and a bottle of water set out on the coffee table, Josh continued reading, gobbling a slice of pie down as he did.

The phone rang.

Josh gave it a drowsy glance and paused in his studying, chewing as he listened.

"Josh. I know you're home and screening your calls. Please pick up. Please?"

"Luis! Get the fucking hint." Josh continued eating. The sound of the line disconnecting followed and his answering machine clicked off. Shaking his head at Luis' tenacity, or stupidity, Josh finished his second slice, brushed off his hands, and kept working.

By ten o'clock, he had enough of the damn books. He memorized everything he thought he needed to know for the exams. With medical terminology spinning through his head, he washed up the dish he'd used, wrapped up the leftover pizza, stuck it in the fridge, and crushed up the box.

Going through his evening routine, Josh cleaned up for bed and knelt beside his television in his bedroom. Thumbing through his collection of gay porn, he slipped *Hard Core* into the DVD player and splayed out naked on his sheets, remote control in hand.

Fast forwarding to one of his favorite scenes, Adam Hart naked and hard, Josh released the remote and replaced it with his cock. Watching the gorgeous six-foot tall, blue-eyed blond do his thing, Josh stroked himself slowly at first, until the craving grew too urgent. Tensing his muscles, staring through his own dick at Hart's, Josh came, closing his eyes and milking the cum out with long, slow pulls. Laying his head back on the pillows, Josh took a few moments to recover. Before he fell asleep, he motivated himself, shut off the DVD, and made it to the bathroom to clean up.

Lights off, under the covers, he fell into a deep slumber.

# Chapter Four

Tanner leaned against the wall in the back of the room at Santa Monica's section headquarters as the new recruits were assigned. He was going to mentor one of the newbies on his stretch of beach.

Captain Matthew Anderson was in front of the group, giving out advice and precautions before sending the new flock of lifeguards out for the real test.

Looking over the assembly, seeing it was the usual small percentage of women compared to the men, Tanner assumed he'd be assigned a male.

"And most of all," Captain Anderson continued, "be safe, alert, and don't get distracted."

Another long-term permanent, Joe Carter, leaned against Tanner to whisper, "Nice group."

"It is. Best I've seen for a few months." Tanner scanned the backs of the physically fit bodies.

"I hope a few of them stay on at summer's end."

"It's a tougher job than most of these young people anticipate. It tends to weed them out quickly."

"True."

As the assignments were announced, Tanner paid closer attention to the names. He had already mentally chosen his favorite.

Hearing what he had hoped, Tanner waved the young man over to him when Josh looked his way for instruction. Tanner held the man's paperwork in his hand, and led him out of the noisy building to the white sand and warm breeze.

Before Tanner spoke, another new recruit walked past, touching his recruit's arm.

"Good luck, Josh."

"You too, Emily."

Tanner paused for a moment as the woman walked away. He looked down at Josh who was grinning at him with wild green eyes.

"Hey," Josh said in the awkwardness.

"Hey. Right. Are you ready?" Tanner caught his nod. "Good. Let's go." He started them moving in the direction to his stretch of beach. "So? Are you excited?"

"Yes. I'm pumped."

Glancing sideways at the handsome man, Tanner grinned at his enthusiasm.

"It's already an insane asylum on the beach, Josh. But it gets even worse during the holiday weekends. That's the time the mobs show up."

"It gets bad. I know. I used to be one of the weekend bathers here."

Josh's shoulder brushed his, and Tanner glanced down at him quickly. "Are you intending on being a full-time permanent?"

"I am." Josh beamed at him in excitement.

Though Tanner wasn't attracted to men, he certainly knew an exceptional guy if he bumped into one. Josh was fucking pretty.

"Good. It's nice to find someone who wants to make a career out of it. Most people just work for the summer and leave."

"Yes. I figured that. You only need the extra bodies in the summer."

The sand was warming quickly in the morning sun. Tanner felt Josh brushing against him again. He checked to see if Josh even knew he was walking practically on top of him or if he was just being clumsy.

When it happened again, Tanner asked, "You okay?"

"Yes, why?"

Tanner made an obvious gesture to the way their arms overlapped.

"Maybe I am a little nervous." Josh flashed him a sensual smile and didn't move away.

It sent an odd flutter to Tanner's mid-section. *Christ, if he were a woman, I'd ask him out. Holy fuck.*

"You'll do fine. I remember you from the thousand meter swim. You were one of the top five."

"I try my best." Josh rubbed affectionately against Tanner's side.

*Is this a come on?* Tanner couldn't remember a man acting quite so boldly toward him before.

When they arrived at their tower, he paused to look back at Josh before walking up the wooden ramp. There was so much sensuality and raw attraction in the man's eyes that it made his cock move. Tanner quickly turned and went up the ramp, stunned at his reaction.

In all his thirty fucking years, ten of them spent looking at every shape of semi-clad bodies on a beach, he had never reacted to another man before.

*Holy fuck, I want you.*

Josh could smell Tanner's scent from where he stood. Sweat, coconut sunscreen, and if he leaned close enough, he could swear he could catch a whiff of his balls. Josh had to touch him. It wasn't an option.

He stood by as Tanner unlocked the hut and pointed out a few things. "That's the emergency line. You can call 911 or the dispatch to get a break if you need one...this is the log book..."

Josh pressed up against him from behind as Tanner showed him the paperwork. *Let him move because I'm not.*

"Uh," Tanner stammered, "you...you need to write what you've done for the day here...just...uh, just the event...and if uh, you get...get...the zip code of the victim or contact..."

"Uh huh," Josh said distractedly. The heat of Tanner's body and his scent was driving him insane. He smiled to himself at ruffling the big, muscular hunk. He almost laughed as Tanner continued to stutter like a nervous teenager.

As he turned to point to the cones and the first aid kit, and anything else the hut contained, Josh made sure he had Tanner's attention. Josh gripped the back collar of his t-shirt and pulled it over his head as slowly and seductively as he could. Once it was off, Josh brushed his fingers through his hair and fixed his sunglasses to sit better on his nose.

"Right. Uh..." He nearly smirked, as Tanner tore his gaze off his chest. "Uh...where was I? Oh, right. Man the tower at all times unless you feel it's quiet enough to do sprints or exercises. Use your judgment, obviously, and always take a rescue can with you."

Josh followed Tanner out of the shack again, as he explained. When they stood at the front rail, Josh glanced over at a pair of women walking toward them, most likely on their way to the next tower. It seemed they were scoping him and Tanner out as they neared.

Seeing the typical California babe type, Josh focused on the man next to him and imagined those women would be very hot for a man as gorgeous as Tanner. The guy was most likely beating them off with a stick.

"And...uh...make sure you let someone know if you need a break and drink plenty of water, especially if the temperature gets in the nineties."

Josh rubbed his hand over his crotch. He was getting a fucking hard-on staring at the man. *Jesus. What? Six-two? Six-three? Look at the arms on the guy. I need mouth-to-mouth resuscitation please.*

"Okay, Josh, do you have any questions?"

Josh woke up at the sound of his name. "No." *Other than, will you go out with me?*

The women approached them on their way. "Hey, Tanner."

"Hi, Destiny, Samantha," he greeted them. "This is Josh."

"Hi, Josh!"

"Hey," he replied without enthusiasm. *Ooh, you two are regular Baywatch chicks. Whoopee.*

"Poor Tanner. Did you get stuck mentoring?" Samantha winked at him.

"I don't mind." He smiled back and Josh rolled his eyes in annoyance.

"Bye, Tanner! Just signal if you need us for anything." Destiny waved.

"I will. Thanks."

Under his breath, Josh muttered, "Bye-bye." Watching them walk away, Josh noticed one of the two give the object of his desire goo-goo eyes and a slight purse of her lips. Immediately, Josh twisted back to see Tanner's reaction. Expecting him to be throwing her kisses, he was surprised to see Tanner staring in another direction.

*Oh really?* Josh smirked. *A friend of Dorothy? Could I be that lucky?*

"Here."

Josh felt something touch his shoulder. He turned around to find Tanner holding out the binoculars. Since Tanner was standing close again, Josh deliberately brushed against him as he took them. "Thanks, Tanner." He took a deep inhale of Tanner's scent as he did. "Where's the sunscreen?"

When Tanner disappeared into the hut, Josh hurried behind him. He didn't want to miss another opportunity to get the man alone in the interior of the shack.

Standing at the opening of the door, Josh pushed his sunglasses to the top of his head in the dim interior shade, staring at Tanner's ass as he knelt down by a drawer of a long, horizontal cabinet. Josh closed the gap between them.

Tanner made a move to stand, but he found himself posed in front of Josh's crotch. The red fabric of his swim trunks was slightly tented by a large erection. Tanner raised his eyes to Josh's face. The expression on Josh was hypnotic. His light eyes seemed lit from behind. His dark brown hair was thick and shaggy and covered his ears and forehead.

As Tanner rose to his full height, he noticed Josh's gaze followed his.

"Here." He handed him the sun block.

"Thanks."

Tanner felt a surge of electricity as Josh touched his hand to take it. He had an urge to jerk away. Coming back to himself, he ordered, "Get outside and keep watch."

"Yes, sir." Josh's smile only made him more appealing.

Releasing his grasp on the tube of sunscreen, Tanner held his breath as he watched him leave. There was an extra swoosh to his hips as if he knew he was staring at his ass. Before he left the hut, Josh paused and looked back over his shoulder. Tanner thought the gesture was so damn sexy his heart began to pound.

Another wicked grin aimed his way, and Josh left.

Tanner took a moment to recuperate. *What the fuck was that?* He'd worked with several gay men before. All of them knew he was straight and none made any kind of move on him. And he hadn't expected they would. Tanner was a permanent, he earned their respect and they earned his. Holding out his hand, seeing it tremble, Tanner realized in the past that finger on his left hand held a golden ring. There was no ring now.

Staring at the open door and its bright sunlight, Tanner forced himself to calm down before he left the shady hut.

Josh rubbed the sun block on his chest and shoulders. As he massaged the lotion into his skin, he caught Tanner coming out of the hut. *What took you so long, big boy? Taming your hard-on?*

Josh stared directly at Tanner's crotch as he coated himself with cream. "Can you do my back?" Josh asked boldly. Moving closer to the big guy, he smoothed his hands over his chest, keeping his hungry stare on Tanner. *One week and I'll be sucking your cock.*

Seeing his hesitation, Josh could tell Tanner was about to refuse. "Just a little. I burn easy." Josh handed over the cream.

He suppressed a pleased smile when Tanner took the bottle and blobbed some in his palm and waited.

Josh spun around, dying to feel this god's hands on him. At the first touch, Josh melted down to his toes.

༄༅

It shouldn't have been a big deal. He'd certainly spread sun block on people before. Just not on one who was so overtly interested. Not a man who was anyway.

He couldn't help but notice Josh's skin was hot and silky. Tanner tried to finish quickly so it wouldn't seem as if he liked it. Josh's sexy moans, and his wriggling as he touch him made Tanner's breath catch in his throat. *Jesus! What the hell is going on?*

Tanner stopped, wiping the residual cream on his own legs to get rid of the stickiness.

He tried ignoring the seductive look Josh gave him over his shoulder.

"Thanks. Shall I *do you?*"

"I'm good." Tanner took the tube back to the hut. Once he set it back into the drawer, he had to take a minute to calm down.

༄༅

Toward mid-day the crowd grew and the sun blazed high in the sky.

Josh relaxed next to Tanner on the rail as they surveyed the water and shore diligently.

"Are you hungry, Josh?"

"A little." Josh leaned against his arm as if they had already established that boundary. "Why? Are you?"

"I just thought if you wanted to eat your lunch…"

"Okay." Josh headed to the hut and took his sandwich out of his backpack. Carrying it to the front of the tower where Tanner was standing with the binoculars at his eyes, Josh asked, "Bite?"

Tanner looked down at him curiously.

"Avocado and cucumber, mm!" Josh held it up for Tanner. "You'll like it."

Before Tanner could reply, Destiny showed up at their tower. "Either of you guys need a break, Tanner?"

"No. We're good."

Josh caught her gaze and felt like sticking out his tongue at her. He could tell she liked Tanner by her less than subtle body language.

"You sure?"

"Yes. Thanks, Destiny."

"Here." Josh offered Tanner his sandwich. "Have a bite."

Tanner looked uneasy. That made Josh even more excited. *He's worried. Good. That means he's attracted.*

It seemed as if Tanner was waiting for Destiny to leave before he made any decision.

"Fine. See ya later." She walked off in what Josh would call 'a huff'. It made him grin with satisfaction.

Now Tanner was free to take the offered bite.

Josh fed it to him, nudging Tanner's hand aside as he reached for it.

"Good." Tanner nodded as he chewed.

"Take half," Josh suggested.

"I can't eat your lunch. I brought my own."

"I don't mind. We can share." Josh smiled sweetly at him, handing him half of the sandwich. They both ate quietly.

"So, uh," Tanner stuttered nervously, "what…uh…what did you used to do, before this job?"

"I was an office manager. Hated it." Josh brushed against Tanner's arm again lightly.

"You do realize how hard being a lifeguard is." Tanner looked at Josh.

Josh stared back at him.

Tanner devoured the rest of the sandwich, brushed off his hands, and stepped back. "Look. I'm going to say something here and I don't want you to get offended."

"Oh?" Josh felt his stomach flutter in excitement.

"Yes. With all the political correctness nowadays, I feel like I can't say anything without getting a beef."

"Go ahead. Feel free." Josh turned to face Tanner full on.

"I'm not gay."

"I love it when men tell me that." Josh grinned wickedly at him. "It's such a turn-on."

"I'm serious, Josh."

"That's a shame."

"I'm really sorry."

"No. It's a shame for you."

Tanner glanced at him again and quickly replied, "A shame for me?"

"Yes. I give great head."

Tanner shifted his body weight from leg to leg.

Josh touched Tanner's arm, and whispered his words, making them more intimate to keep his attention. "I would have sucked you so deep and hard, you'd think your balls were in my throat." Josh paused seeing a slight bulge appear under Tanner's red swimsuit. "And I swallow."

Tanner choked, coughing to cover his gasp of surprise.

Josh added, "And you don't have to call me afterwards…unless you want me to suck it again. And you will. Believe me."

Josh watched Tanner's skin rise with goose bumps and his dick was growing under his red suit.

Tanner backed up and stared at the beach. In the ensuing pause, Josh finished his lunch and took pleasure in catching Tanner glancing back at him.

As Tanner worried, Josh was beaming. He knew damn well once he got his lips around Tanner's cock, Tanner would be at his mercy. He'd never turned a straight man, but most of his gay videos had that theme. Seducing the heterosexual macho man and converting him into a gay sex fiend. Delicious.

His lunch eaten, Josh stood behind Tanner as he focused on the populated coast. Josh jolted as Tanner accidentally stepped backward into him. Using the opportunity, Josh cupped Tanner's bottom and moved him aside gently.

"Sorry," Tanner whispered.

"My pleasure." Josh allowed his hand to linger on Tanner's perfect butt before he removed it.

"I'm going to get my lunch."

"Okay." Josh watched as he escaped. *Oh well, nothing ventured nothing gained.*

---

The offer of sexual release was weighing on him. Tanner knew interacting with the staff on any level wasn't a good idea, and letting Josh suck his dick was right up there with one of the worst scenarios he could imagine. No way. That could never happen. But *holy shit*, why was he even thinking about it?

Tanner tried not to imagine a good, satisfying blowjob. Anna didn't like doing it. She had done it once before they got married, but didn't swallow. Tanner assumed it was something women didn't enjoy and chalked it up to the stuff of fantasies.

---

The long day done and dusted, back at his apartment, Josh felt hot and tired. Tossing his small backpack onto the counter, he headed to the shower to cool off and scrub the sand and lotion off his skin.

Under the spray, closing his eyes, Josh imagined what it would be like to kiss a man like Tanner. A soft moan echoed off the wet tile. He wondered if he would ever find out.

Using the soap, Josh made his body slippery and moved out from under the running water. Dragging his palm over the length of his soft cock, it hardened with both his actions and his thoughts. Envisioning making love to a man like Tanner, so masculine and straight, made Josh's skin light on fire. "Oh, what I would do to you," he moaned. "You'd be so incredible to squirm on." Josh opened his lips as his dick became thicker and more sensitive to his touch. Widening his stance, Josh wished he were licking Tanner's. "Yes…" Josh felt a wave of pleasure rush over his length. "Let me suck it, Tanner…"

Imagining the scent of Tanner's skin and sweat wash over him, his balls tensed up and he came. His cum emerging in creamy roping streams, Josh grunted and milked himself gently. "Oh, Tanner…what I would give to taste your spunk. Augh!"

Josh dried himself and stared in the foggy mirror for a moment. He wiped a ring off the dewy glass so he could see himself and stared at his face critically. "Am I pretty enough for you, Tanner? Hm?"

Tossing the towel over the shower door, Josh spread shaving foam on his jaw and quickly got rid of his growing beard. He brushed his hair and gazed at himself. "Better than those beach bimbos."

Josh shook himself out of his thoughts and frustration and left the bathroom. He slipped on a pair of shorts, and hunted down food. As he prepared a meal, the phone rang. Wishing it was Tanner, knowing exactly who it was, Josh frowned and set the pan off the burner. He stared down at the caller ID and rolled his eyes.

"What," he said into the receiver.

"Josh, see me."

"Luis. Are you stupid or what?"

"I'm going crazy. Please."

Josh walked back to his frying pan, stirred his omelet and set it back on the burner. "Luis, I can't. You'll just hurt me again. You have to move on."

"Please! Joshua!"

"Don't know what ya got until ya lose it. Typical."

"Yeah, well, maybe."

"I'm sorry, Luis. I can't."

"The guys miss you here at work. You could at least stop by."

"Can't. I'm too busy." He shut off the burner and stared at his dinner. "I've just made a meal for myself. Can I eat it or will you keep bugging me?"

"I'll keep bugging you."

Josh dropped the phone on the kitchen counter, scooped his food onto a plate and sat down at the table.

"Hello? You there?" Luis called over the line.

Josh picked up the phone again. "You are a pain in the ass."

"In a good way?"

"You used to be in a good way, now you're just an ass."

"Baby, we meant so much to each other."

"Then why did you cheat on me?" Josh ate quickly he was so hungry.

"It was a momentary lapse of reason."

"What are you, Pink Floyd? Where do you come up with this stuff?"

"You've never cheated on someone? Come on, Josh. Everyone cheats."

"No, Luis, contrary to popular belief, not everyone cheats."

"Bull shit."

Josh finished his meal and pushed the plate aside. As he stared into his living room, he exhaled deeply. "I always figure it this way, Luis."

"Yes, Joshua?"

"If you feel the need to go with someone else, then it's over. Right?"

"No. Not necessarily."

"Was our sex bad?" Josh knew damn well he gave good head and was a perfect bottom.

"Bad? Are you nuts?"

"Then why cheat? You see my point?"

"Baby, how many times can I apologize?"

"As many times as you'd like. I still won't take you back." Josh stood and set his plate in the sink.

"One more chance."

"No. Luis, move on."

"I can't."

"You can. Let me go. This conversation is getting you nowhere and me pissed off."

"Don't go."

"Bye, Luis." Josh hung up and tossed the phone back on the counter as he washed the dishes. "Why do they all want me back once they screw me up? Huh?"

He rested the dish and frying pan in the drain board, drying his hands. Yeah, the easy route would be to go back with Luis. Chasing Tanner was going to end up being a lost cause. The guy is straight.

Josh dropped onto the sofa and pointed the remote control at the TV, trying to forget everything for a few hours before bed. It was all just too frustrating to deal with at the moment.

# Chapter Five

Josh got ready for his first Saturday shift early. He had been warned the weekends were much more manic than the weekdays. Nothing had happened on his first day to use any of his rescue skills, and Josh wasn't happy about it. He wanted the practice. He'd heard the horror stories from the trainers at the fire department. Eleven rescues on Memorial Day last year. It was enough to get his nerves going.

He stuffed his mobile phone, wallet, and his lunch into his pack. Josh slung it over his shoulder, grabbed his keys, and locked his door. The underground parking area was cool from the overnight drop in temperature. Climbing into his car, using the power convertible button, he waited for the soft top to fold back. His sunglasses on his nose, imagining Tanner sitting next to him on the soft, cloth seat, Josh left the shady parking garage behind and hit the rising temperatures of the tarmac and cloudless sky.

While the radio blasted Travis' *Why Does It Always Rain On Me?*, Josh wondered what Tanner did last night. He had no idea if the man was dating, engaged, divorced, or married with children and didn't wear a ring…no clue.

"Did you think about me? Have I intrigued you? Are you curious at all?" Josh paused at a traffic signal and looked at the car stopped alongside him. A woman was staring blatantly at him. When their gazes caught, she smiled amiably. Josh smiled back. Just as her window began descending for what Josh imagined was communication, the light changed and he took off. "Sorry, not interested."

Tanner sat in his white Jeep Wrangler, starting up the engine. Feeling the heat already present in the morning air, he fastened his seatbelt, his soft-top roof already off, allowing the breeze to flow around him as he drove. Imagining the hefty crowds on a beautiful summer Saturday, Tanner knew it was going to be chaos on the beach.

On the drive, his mind wandered to Josh. He hated to admit he was giving his offer some consideration. It was absolutely ludicrous, but…

He thought about his other options—and cringed. Women needed commitment and security. What Tanner wanted was sexual release with no strings attached.

Did the idea of having a man suck his dick gross him out? That was the question. Normally, yes. But…

Josh Elliot was certainly an exception to the rule and a better choice than finding some slut to screw at a bar. He couldn't do that for many reasons. Yet, that's what he craved. Sex only.

If he allowed Josh to blow him, would there be expectations of more? And what were they if there was? Tanner assumed he would not have to reciprocate. He didn't think he could. Put a dick in his mouth? No way.

Parking behind section headquarters, Tanner shut off his car. A red convertible eased in beside him.

As he climbed out of his jeep, Tanner realized it was Josh. Seeing him topless in the snazzy automobile, Tanner couldn't help but admire him. The man was fantastic. And his confidence and intelligence were like beacons blazing out from him. It made Josh very appealing in so many ways.

"Hey, boss." Josh grinned flirtatiously.

"Josh," Tanner replied, waiting as Josh exited his car.

"Did you have a nice night?" Josh approached him, moving inside Tanner's aura, much closer than any casual acquaintance ever would. Tanner caught a whiff of his cologne or masculine deodorant.

"Any wild orgies? Drunken binges?" Josh teased. "Porn videos?"

Tanner couldn't help but smile at his charisma. "Why do I get the feeling you are a very naughty man?"

"Oh? Do I give off that vibe?" Josh acted amazed. "Or is that just wishful thinking on your part?"

"You do know I'm straight." Tanner felt as if he had to keep reminding him.

"You told me that yesterday." Josh licked his lips slowly, lowering his gaze from under his sunglasses to Tanner's crotch, briefly. "I assume you're either reminding yourself, or...trying to excite me."

Tanner took a quick look at his watch as well as the area in close proximity to make sure they weren't overheard. "Even if I were gay, relationships at work are risky." A strange cloud passed over Josh's face, as if Tanner had said something to strike a chord. "But I'm not gay."

The brilliant smile returned to Josh's face. "I'm amazed at how many times you're repeating that. Are you playing hard to get? Because you're turning me on."

For some reason that made Tanner break up with laughter. "What am I going to do with you?"

"Give us an hour alone, big boy, and I'll fill you in."

"Go." Tanner nudged Josh to the building.

"Oh...you bully. Pushing me around. Ah! Do it again!"

"Get going, trouble-maker," Tanner scolded playfully, shaking his head at Josh's antics.

❧❦

Once they had checked the information board to get their assignments, they walked to their tower. Josh dumped his things off inside the hut and coated his arms and face in sunscreen.

"Hey."

He turned around and found Samantha, another permanent assigned to their tower on and off during his mentoring. She put a water bottle and her lunch on the counter.

"Need help with that?"

"Huh?" Josh paused and looked at the lotion in his hand. "Uh, sure." He'd rather have Tanner do it, but knew it would seem odd to ask him since Sam had offered.

She took the tube from him and squeezed some out into her palm as Josh continued to rub it into his face and neck. The first touch of the cool cream on his back made his skin tingle. Closing his eyes, visualizing Tanner, Josh fell into a nice little daydream.

"I've been in this job for two years now," Samantha said, "and I've seen a lot of guys, Josh…"

Josh waited for her to finish her sentence. "And? But? Is there more to this story?" She relinquished her touch as she set the cream on the counter and wiped her hands off on a paper towel.

"I shouldn't say anything more. I guess it'll either make me sound dumb or swell your head."

Josh retrieved the sun cream and used it to coat his chest and abs. He looked up at Sam to see she was gazing dreamily at him. Tanner stepped into the hut behind her.

"Sam?" Tanner asked. "Why don't you go out outside and keep an eye on things?"

"Okay," Samantha replied. She passed Tanner at the doorway and hissed, "Christ, he's gorgeous."

Josh heard the comment, looking at Tanner, still massaging the sun cream into his skin. Tanner was staring at him and his focus seemed to be bypassing Josh instead of on him. "Where do you want me, Tanner?" Josh whispered seductively, his hand dipping into the front of his red swimsuit.

It snapped Tanner out of his thoughts. "Take a walk down the beach. Bring a rescue buoy with you. It's going to be a hot, packed, busy day today. And I know we're in for some problems."

Josh saluted him. "Yes, sir."

Tanner left. Josh moaned in agony. *Let me suck it. Come on.*

❧

Tanner stood next to Samantha on the tower as Josh removed a buoy from the rail. Josh turned back to look at him as he left. Tanner felt a slight flutter in his gut. While the rest of the newbies were salivating over the female staff, the female staff was leering at Josh. How ironic was that?

"Christ, he so pretty." Samantha let out a loud burst of air with her comment.

Tanner glanced over at her as she used the binoculars to watch Josh, not the growing crowd.

"Does he have a girlfriend?" Samantha asked. "I want to ask him out. I'm just giving him a couple of days to settle in first." She nudged him. "Tanner? Do you know anything about Josh?"

"Not really." Tanner located two other new recruits, Christopher and Noah, with their mentors, doing sprints on the hard packed sand before his attention went back to Josh moving along the length of the beach.

"How old is he?" Samantha inquired.

"Twenty-six." Tanner had the answer to that question. He knew Josh's age from his paperwork.

"He must have a girlfriend." Samantha leaned her forearms on the rail. "Or he'd at least flirt with me."

Tanner laughed under his breath. "I'm going to take a walk and look around."

"Okay, Tanner." Samantha put the binoculars back to her eyes.

"Make sure you look at something other than Josh, okay?" Tanner said with a slight hint of seriousness to make his point.

"It'll be hard, but I will," she teased.

❧❧

Josh carried the plastic can, swinging it as he walked.

He met up with another recruit from the next tower who was heading his way on his patrol.

"Josh!"

"Hey, Nat." They exchanged handshakes.

"How's your mentorship going?"

"Good." Josh nodded.

"Christ, look at all these chicks." Nathan peered over his dark sunglasses.

"You should do well, Nat. All the girls love a lifeguard."

"Me? Jesus, Josh, they're all drooling over you."

"They're barking up the wrong tree with me." Josh scanned the rough surf.

"How's that?" Nathan seemed to be barely listening, too busy ogling.

"Never mind." Moving closer to the water, away from the blankets, folding chairs, and umbrellas, they joined ranks for a few minutes. They skirted around moats where children dug holes around sandcastles quickly flooded by the incoming tide. Josh kept his vision out at the water. He paused a moment to watch someone.

"What?" Nathan asked.

"Hang on." Josh slowly unraveled the harness on the buoy. "Shit." He felt an adrenalin dump as it appeared someone needed help.

"Is she for real or just pretending?" Nathan asked, stepping closer to the water.

"I don't think we can wait to find out." Josh looped the harness over his head, diagonally across his chest, and took off running. He speared into the water, dragging the plastic can behind him, and swam out to the distressed swimmer. She was flailing her arms and dunking under the waves.

He tossed the buoy to her as he was trained and shouted, "Grab the can!"

She didn't respond to his commands. He closed in on her and wrapped around her torso under her pink halter-top bikini.

"You got her?" Nathan asked, gasping, as it appeared his nerves kicked in.

"Yeah." Josh held onto her, swimming to the beach as several people stopped to watch.

Josh held her under the arms from behind and brought her to dry sand. He laid her down gently, the plastic buoy dragging behind him. Nathan checked her neck. "She has a pulse."

Josh leaned down to see if she was breathing, watching her chest for movement. With his ear to her lips, he was suddenly grabbed around the shoulders and kissed. He jerked backward to gape at her and found her silly smirk.

"I need mouth-to-mouth, you beautiful hunk!" she moaned dramatically.

"That's not funny!" Josh wrenched out of her grip. "You think it's a joke but it's a very serious offense! While you're being stupid someone else could be drowning." Josh stood, glaring down at her, the saline dripping from his wet hair down his face and back.

"Jeez. Calm down." The woman sat up. "I just wanted to meet you."

Someone touched Josh's shoulder. He thought it was Nathan but found Tanner, soaked in sweat and panting from his sprint. "You all right?"

"Yeah. I'm just pissed as shit." Josh gestured to the woman. "She pretended she was drowning. Some joke." He looked up and found a crowd had gathered. It was humiliating suddenly to have been duped, like he and Nathan should have realized it was a ruse. But he couldn't take that chance.

Tanner crouched down next to her. "It's a criminal offense, miss. False reporting."

"Oh! I didn't mean anything by it." Her humor soon turned to fear. "I just thought he was adorable and didn't think he would talk to me if I just walked up to him."

Tanner glanced up at Josh. "You want me to get the police?"

"No. Forget it." Josh felt his cheeks get rosy and walked away, wrapping up the buoy as he did, taking the harness off.

Nathan caught up to him, keeping him from running off. "Wow. I'd be really flattered if a chick did that for me, Josh."

"I'm gay. Okay?" Josh snapped at him, immediately feeling bad. "Sorry. I didn't mean to shout at you."

Nathan's mouth hung open in shock. "You're gay?"

Josh turned to look over his shoulder to see Tanner. He was still lecturing the girl. Since they weren't getting her arrested, Josh figured they at least owed her and the gawkers a stern warning.

Once Tanner told her to leave the beach, he walked over to where he and Nathan were lingering near the water.

"You two did an outstanding job." Tanner put his hand on Josh's shoulder. "I watched it from the beginning and you were spot on target in your procedure."

"I feel like an idiot." Josh glanced over Tanner's shoulder as people continued to stare at them.

"No. You did exactly what you should have done."

Nathan was gaping at Josh, his jaw slack from the impact of Josh's admission. Seeing his expression, Josh slapped Nathan in the chest with the back of his hand. "Get over it!"

Tanner appeared confused. "What's going on? Did you react badly to the rescue?"

"No. Nothing like that. Never mind," Nathan mumbled.

"Come on." Tanner put his arm around Josh's shoulder as they walked.

Josh waved. "See ya later, Nat."

"I'm going your way, Josh."

"Oh. Okay."

Nathan fell in beside them.

Josh was so preoccupied he didn't even realize Tanner was holding onto him until they were a few yards down the beach. The moment he did, he reacted, putting his around Tanner's waist.

Josh caught someone leering as they walked by. "What are you looking at?" he sneered.

The young man quickly turned away.

Josh loved holding Tanner. He knew it was Tanner's way of showing his support, his confidence, and his pride in him, but Josh wished it was more. Tightening his hold on Tanner's hip, Josh pressed his fingers against Tanner's muscles, feeling them flex as he walked.

※※

Tanner was so impressed with Josh's first rescue and his professional ability, he was beaming. The fact it had been a fake damsel in distress, though illegal and annoying, amused Tanner. Who knew what lengths a woman would go to get her claws into a man like Josh Elliot? Tanner had a feeling false alarms around this man would become a regular habit.

As Josh wrapped his arm around his hip, Tanner wondered what it would look like to Nathan, or to Samantha, who undoubtedly had the binoculars trained on them as they approached. It felt natural. He was Josh's mentor.

Feeling Josh's fingers press into his skin, Tanner knew Josh was showing him his attraction. At this point, Tanner thought it was endearing and savored it.

"What happened?" Samantha asked as they drew closer.

Tanner dropped his arm from Josh's shoulder. "A young woman thought drowning would be more effective than a pick-up line."

Samantha smiled wickedly at Josh. "I have a feeling that won't be the last woman to fake it so you'll give her mouth-to-mouth resuscitation, hot stuff."

"I felt like an idiot." Josh dropped his arm from Tanner's hip and hung his rescue buoy back on the rail.

"Don't. It's a compliment, Josh." Samantha walked down the ramp and pecked his cheek. "Because you're gorgeous."

"Stop." Josh blushed nudging her away.

"And gay."

They all spun around to look at Nathan.

"Nat!" Josh scolded. "I think it's up to me to make that announcement."

Tanner felt horrible for Josh instantly and checked the expression of surprise on Samantha's face. "Go." He nudged Samantha. "Do some sprints."

Tanner craned his finger at Nathan. "A word," he admonished, gesturing to the hut. "Are you going to be all right, Josh?" Tanner handed him the binoculars.

"Yeah." Josh walked up the ramp and leaned on the rail, facing the water.

"Be right back." Tanner gave Nathan's shoulder a light shove to urge him to go first. Alone with Nathan, Tanner folded his arms across his chest and waited for eye contact. "Who's your mentor, Nat?"

"Joe Carter."

Tanner intended to let Joe know about the incident. "With your rescue training you had a course in diversity, didn't you?"

"I didn't mean anything by it, Tanner. Josh is all right."

"You had no right to just blurt that out."

"I know. It's just that I figured if Sam knew he was gay, she'd leave him alone. We had a course in sexual harassment too, Tanner."

"Josh is a full grown man and can defend himself. If he didn't like something he would say it." Tanner knew damn well Nathan only announced it because he was jealous of the attention Josh was getting. There was no comparison in beauty between the two. Tanner also assumed Nathan was hot to trot for his fellow female lifeguards, possibly even Samantha.

"Sorry, Tanner."

"I'm not the one you need to be apologizing to."

"I know."

"If I hear you've been gossiping about him again, I'll have you kicked out of here. I know Joe would back me up." Tanner felt miserable for Josh. Poor guy. Two days into his mentorship and outted by a boney, jealous jerk. That had to be rough.

∽∾

The hot sun had completely dried Josh's hair and bathing suit. Though it had been a false alarm, Josh was glad, in a way, he'd had his first rescue. He wasn't sure how he'd react in a real situation, and the fact that his training had kicked in was a huge relief. It amazed him that a woman could be so naïve to think that was a way to seduce a man. It showed her lack of respect for his job and the safety of everyone else on the beach.

Hearing a soft echo of a voice coming from the hut behind him, Josh thought about Nathan exposing his secret. In a place deep inside, he was glad. It saved him the trouble of making any type of announcement, and hopefully, would keep the advances of his female co-workers at bay. Josh just wondered what Tanner thought of his sexual preference being common knowledge. He was afraid Tanner would dread mentoring him because of guilt by association. And that would suck.

Nathan approached him. "Sorry, man."

Josh took his outstretched hand. "It's all right, Nat."

"Nat, get back to your tower and tell Joe I need to speak to him at the end of the shift."

"Okay," Nat responded flatly, walking off.

Josh looked back, as Tanner drew near him.

Josh waited, feeling Tanner's body heat, resisting the urge to cop a feel once he was within groping range.

"Are you okay?"

"Hm?" Josh glanced at Tanner's muscled chest. "Me?"

"Yes, you."

Josh closed the space between them. He stood directly in front of Tanner, his five-foot-ten-inch form feeling slightly dwarfed by Tanner's height. Josh very lightly touched Tanner's sternum with the tip of his index finger. "Wanna know what I'm really afraid of?"

"I do."

Through his finger, Josh felt the words vibrate in Tanner's broad chest. "That if people know about me, you'll stop mentoring me." He drew a tiny circle on Tanner's skin.

"I won't do that."

"No? No guilt by association?" Josh drew a line to Tanner's nipple, pressing it like a button with his fingertip.

"I'm not that insecure about my manhood."

"No. I think if you were insecure, you'd certainly punch my lights out for touching you this way." Josh continued his line, drawing down Tanner's rippling muscles to his belly button.

"I know you're just doing it to get a rise out of me."

"Hell yeah." Josh fucked Tanner's navel with his index finger.

"Not that kind of rise."

"Says you." Josh touched Tanner's skin with the tip of his tongue.

This time Tanner stepped back.

"You know you taste as good as you smell." Josh licked his lips.

"I take it by your behavior that you've gotten over the comment from Nat and the little stint on the beach to get your attention."

"Tanner." Josh closed the gap between them again so he could whisper. "If you think little things like that rattle me for long, you don't know me at all."

"No. I don't know you very well."

"Want to get to know me better?" Josh imagined a long, wet lick across Tanner's skin. "Think at all about my offer? A nice, slow, intense blowjob? No strings attached?"

A chuckle emerged from Tanner. "Get your focus back on your job."

Deliberately moving near enough to touch, Josh brushed his crotch against Tanner's, making their semi-hard dicks ride over each other. Josh was stunned Tanner didn't jerk back and run for cover. Tanner boldly withstood the contact. It sent a zing to Josh's groin he was hoping echoed in Tanner. Resisting the urge to grind against him like a bitch in heat, Josh returned to the front of the tower, pushed his sunglasses to the top of his head and raising the binoculars to his eyes.

Samantha rejoined them.

Josh gave her the binoculars.

"Thanks." She took them and spoke as she gazed through them, "Can I ask you a question, Josh?"

"Yes, Sam." He smiled shyly.

"Have you always been gay?"

"Yup." He rolled his sunglasses back down his nose.

"Ever been with a woman?"

"Nope."

"Do your mom and dad know?"

"Yup." Josh smiled at her. "What? Am I the first gay guy you've had a chance to interview?"

"Yup." Samantha hit him with her hip playfully.

"Go on, ask me anything." Josh grinned, feeling Tanner's presence behind him, knowing he was listening.

"What's it feel like having a man make love to you?"

"Fucking amazing." Josh scanned the beach.

Samantha leaned closer, hissing, "Do you actually suck guys' cocks?"

"Oh yes." Josh was dying to see Tanner's expression.

"Do you like that too?"

"Mm," Josh hummed, nodding his head.

"Do you have a boyfriend now?"

"No. Not at the moment." Unable to resist, Josh looked over his shoulder. Tanner was indeed there, listening but gazing at the crowd dutifully. Goading Samantha, Josh elbowed her. "Ask me something else."

"Uh…do you like kissing guys too?"

"Love it."

"Wow, Josh. I can't imagine a guy kissing you. It's so weird."

"Not to me." Josh glanced at Tanner, parting his lips sensuously.

Tanner turned beet red even though he was pretending not to listen.

Josh smiled wickedly and continued to survey the crowd. "Tanner?"

"Hm?" Tanner walked up behind them as if he hadn't been able to hear every word they said.

"How the hell do you check on each person in a crowd like this?"

"Look for movement that's unusual. And I do tend to keep the bathers in the water as a priority. People can't drown on the beach."

"Okay." Josh scanned back and forth for a few minutes before Samantha handed him the binoculars. Josh spun around to see Tanner. He was gazing out at the sea like a movie star in a beach movie. "Do you attend recertifying classes, Tanner?"

"Yes. Once a month everyone does."

*Good.* Josh was hoping they could go on those together. It would at least be a chance to hang out with him once the mentorship was over and they parted ways.

A seasonal staff member relieved them at eight. Josh gathered his belongings and began walking back to section headquarters with Tanner and Samantha. While they strolled, Josh brushed against Tanner. Then as discreetly as he could, Josh smoothed down the line of muscle on the side of Tanner's leg with his fingertips, petting the fine brown hair slowly.

Tanner glanced down but didn't brush his hand away.

They returned to headquarters to check on their posted assignments. Waiting for Tanner as he took care of his own business inside, which included speaking to Joe Carter, Nathan's mentor, Josh loitered by the cement stairs leading to street level. Leaning back against the handrail, Josh crossed his arms over his bare chest.

"See ya tomorrow, Josh. Sorry about before." Nathan waved.

"It's okay. No big deal, Nat. See ya." Josh smiled at him, seeing Samantha leave without waving or bidding him a farewell. It was possible even though she acted interested she was disappointed in the news that he didn't like women. If that were the case, there was nothing he could do about it.

Tanner emerged from the building. Josh stood off the rail and watched his approach. Tanner appeared surprised to see him there. "You need something, Josh?"

"Are you kidding?" Josh laughed at the absurdity of the question, ascending the flight of stairs with him to their cars.

"I meant work related." Tanner gave him a sly grin.

"Okay. Can I work on your cock?"

"Do you pursue all men this hard?"

"Just the straight ones." Josh laughed and added, "No. I don't. Usually they pursue me."

"That I would believe."

"So, uh, can I follow you to your place?" Josh closed in on him again. "I promise it'll be a blowjob you'll never forget."

"That's an understatement." Tanner looked around the area.

"Oh? Tempted?" Josh felt his body light on fire.

"We work together, Josh. I'm your mentor. With all the shit they push at us about sexual harassment—"

Josh stopped him with an index finger to his lips. "Don't even go there. That's a non-issue."

Tanner moved Josh's hand away from his face. "Josh…"

"Tanner," Josh hissed teasingly. "It's your turn to say, 'Josh' again."

Though he was grinning, Tanner shook his head. "I can't."

"Ever have your balls sucked?" Josh moved closer. "Wet and rolling in a mouth?" He noticed Tanner's chest move faster with his growing respirations. "Or a tongue on your ring?"

"Oh, shit…" Tanner stepped back. "I have to get home."

Josh watched his hasty retreat into his jeep. It made him smile. If Tanner wasn't interested, he wouldn't be nearly as nervous. Seeing Tanner back up and drive away, Josh sighed. "I'm getting to you. I know I'm getting to you."

∽∼

Tanner was hard as a rock. He looked in his rear view mirror to see Josh still standing there, gazing after him. Tanner shifted in the driver's seat and pushed his cock between his legs to get it to relax. *Suck my balls? Lick my ass? Oh, my fucking God.*

Imagining that gorgeous creature lapping between his thighs was driving him insane. And the conversation he overheard between Josh and Samantha still haunted him.

*"What's it feel like having a man make love to you?"*

*"Fucking amazing."*

*"Do you actually suck guys' cocks?"*

*"Oh yes."*

*"Do you like that too?"*

*"Mm."*

*"Do you like kissing guys too?"*

*"Love it."*

Tanner couldn't stop touching himself. He was going insane. Though he'd met other gay men, he did not know one personally, and had never heard a man speak so candidly about his feelings.

The fact that Josh was so incredible looking wasn't helping matters. Josh was a natural lifesaver. Top notch. Professional. A man Tanner knew would not only get the job done and do it right, he would pick up the slack for those around him who didn't. Josh Elliot was a man's man and the irony of that concept made Tanner crazy. Gay guys were supposed to be effeminate, soft, limp wristed. None of those adjectives described Josh.

Tanner parked in his driveway at his house in Hawthorne. He hopped out of his car, entered his home, and tossed down the keys and backpack, walking directly to the bathroom and stripping for a cold shower.

Standing under the spray, trying to get control of his libido, Tanner gazed down in disappointment at a cock that stayed hard. "This is crazy. He's a guy!" Tanner closed his eyes in defeat, grabbed his dick and began jacking off. Try as he might, he could not stop thinking about Josh and his seduction.

His dick hadn't been this swollen in ages. Flashes of having his balls sucked, which they never were, or his ass licked, which it never had been, were making Tanner so hot he was shaking as he fisted himself. He kept Josh's gorgeous features in mind and ejaculated, spattering the wet tiles of his shower in thick creamy blobs. Tanner choked he had come so hard, milking his cock gently as more cum oozed out of the slit.

"Mother-fucker. Lick my ass? Suck my balls?" He leaned against the wall to recover. "My ex would rarely suck my damn dick." He caught his breath and noticed his cum still stuck to the back wall of the shower. Cupping the running water, Tanner rinsed it down the drain and continued his washing up. He shampooed his hair, once again trying to imagine what it would feel like to have someone suck his damn nuts. "Bet it's unbelievable." He used soap to wash himself, running his testicles through his fingers under the soft heated skin. "Damn."

Tanner washed his crack. He pushed just the tip of his index finger against his rim, imagining it was Josh's tongue. Tanner's dick began to swell again. "Son of bitch. What the hell have you done to me, Joshua?" Tanner rinsed off, shutting the taps.

He stood dripping, his head hanging tiredly. Tanner knew the more he was around that gorgeous stud, the harder it would be to resist temptation. He wanted to feel a mouth on his balls, a tongue on his ass.

Tanner figured he'd have to pay a hooker a hell of a lot of money to do those stunts to him. Not that he would ever go to a whore and pay for sex anyway. It repulsed him, not to mention it was illegal.

"Why the hell did you have to be so damn perfect, Josh Elliot? Huh?" Tanner wiped the mirror over the sink and stared into his eyes. He looked as crazy as he felt inside.

"You getting bi-curious? Are you nuts?"

*

Josh headed to the underground lot of his apartment and drove past the front of the building. Luis was standing outside the lobby doors.

*Crap.* Josh parked in his assigned spot and carried his backpack with him. Without hesitation, Josh stormed through the lobby to the front where Luis stood.

The abruptness of the door opening startled Luis.

"What do you want?" Josh asked impatiently.

"To talk."

"We already had a talk. Remember? Me telling you it was over."

"Look at you in your red lifeguard suit!" Luis went for a touch.

Josh swatted Luis' hand away. "I don't know how I can make it any clearer. It's over between us."

"It was one night. That was it."

"One night that I found out about, you mean." Josh looked at the passing traffic on the main road in front of the building.

"No. That was it."

Josh stared at Luis' stiff, short, bleached hair as it stood up from his head, his round John Lennon glasses and business suit. Josh wondered what he had seen in him. Luis couldn't hold a candle to Tanner Cameron. "I'm already seeing another guy."

"No. Please don't say that."

"I am."

"Another lifeguard?"

"Yup."

"How the hell am I supposed to compete with that, Joshua?"

"You can't." Josh folded his arms over his bare chest.

"Do you love him?"

Josh shrugged.

"What's he like?"

"Fucking fabulous."

"I can imagine."

"No. You can't." Josh wished he wasn't lying. "Luis, move on. Find someone else."

"Everyone at Buzzworks says you're coming back in September."

"I don't intend to. I've got an option to do more training and to stay on permanently."

"Permanently?" Luis scoffed. "A full-time lifeguard? Oh, grow up."

"Luis, I'm tired. I need to eat and shower."

"Let me come up."

Josh stopped his progress to the lobby door. "Why can't you just let go? I don't want to get mean or nasty. I'm trying to stay calm and do this politely. But if you keep pushing me, I will get mad."

"We had six months together."

"And you went out on me and ruined it."

"Once!"

Shaking his head, Josh replied, "I can't keep going over the same argument. Goodbye, Luis." Josh backed up into the lobby, making sure he shut the door, locking Luis out. He waited for the elevator, watching Luis decide if he should go or not. As if making the decision for him, Josh shouted through the door, "Yes! Go home!" Josh entered the elevator and pushed number three. He closed his eyes as he waited for the door to slide shut. It wasn't his fault the relationship ended. He had been the loyal one.

Coming through his apartment door, Josh felt spent and wondered if this pining over Tanner was only draining him even more than his usual exhaustion. Now he was pretending to have a relationship with him? He must be nuts.

"Tanner is straight! Get over it!" Josh threw his backpack down and headed to the bathroom to wash the salt, sand and tanning lotion off his skin. He stripped and stood waiting for the water to heat. Josh stared at his own cock as it slowly began rising. "Jesus, just thinking about you is making me horny already." Josh groaned in frustration and figured it was another bout of jacking off in the shower to relieve his stress. How long was he supposed to moon over Tanner? An unattainable goal?

"Just forget him and find someone else." Josh stepped under the hot water as his dick stood out from his body like a pole. "Yeah, sure. Someone else." Shaking his head at the futility, Josh once again grabbed his cock, dreamed of Tanner, and gave it the pleasure it craved.

# Chapter Six

Sunday was no better than Saturday. Actually, it was even more crowded. By nine in the morning, people had already begun to set out blankets and umbrellas along the freshly cleaned sand. The roadway adjacent to the beach was filling up with cars cruising up and down the coast.

Josh closed the convertible roof to prevent the sun from burning the interior all day long. While it crept into place over his head, he noticed the white stud-mobile Jeep Wrangler pull up. Having jacked off thinking about him, Josh was already pumped about another day of working with Tanner. Seeing Tanner already on the sidewalk, Josh clipped the roof into place and dashed out to meet him. "Whoa, not so fast, handsome," he teased.

"Good morning, Josh." Tanner smiled sweetly at him. "I trust you behaved yourself last night and didn't get into any mischief."

"Mischief?" Josh pointed to himself. "How could I get into mischief without you around?"

"Somehow I think you would manage."

Josh held Tanner back for a moment to meet his eyes. "No. I wouldn't."

Tanner seemed unprepared for the seriousness of Josh's tone.

"I'm not the type to fuck around, Tanner. Honest."

Blinking in shock, Tanner whispered, "You make it sound as if we're already together and you'd be cheating on me."

In Josh's mind they were. He didn't want anyone else. Was that nuts or what?

"Josh?"

Josh turned away from Tanner's intelligent eyes, suddenly feeling like a fool. Who was he kidding? Tanner was a straight man, and obviously not interested.

&

The light faded from Josh's emerald eyes. Tanner grabbed him as he tried to escape. "Hey. Wait a minute."

Tanner was given the impression that this man was a playboy, happily sucking cocks all night long and it didn't matter whose. Now with this odd conversation, Tanner was getting a different idea. "Josh, look at me."

What had been confidence and lust had changed to shyness. It took a moment, but Josh finally met Tanner's gaze.

"Are you waiting for me?"

Josh tried to shrug out of Tanner's grip but Tanner held on.

"Tell me. Are you imagining us together?"

"Yes. Okay?" Josh's cheeks grew red. "Hey, ya can't blame a guy for trying."

"I'm straight, Josh. Remember?"

"How can I forget?" Josh's wicked smile returned. "I think that's the fourth time you've told me."

Tanner put his arm around Josh's shoulder and urged Josh to walk with him toward headquarters. "I know I keep telling you, but obviously you need reminding."

"Christ, you smell good." Josh held Tanner around the hips and snuffled at his skin.

"You are tenacious, I'll give you that."

Josh licked Tanner's shoulder.

"Now cut that out. Behave," he scolded.

"Are you kidding me? I can't around you. You're my ideal man."

"Really?" Tanner dropped his arm from Josh's shoulder as they walked down the flight of concrete steps.

"Really."

Tanner opened the door to the office allowing Josh to enter first, staring at his ass as he did. *You'd suck my damn balls? Lick my ass?* Tanner moaned in agony. *Why are you a man? Why?*

Tanner asked himself another question, *What am I so afraid of?*

⁂

Once they were at their tower and fell into a routine, Tanner called his name. "Josh."

Josh turned back to the platform surrounding the tower and found Tanner standing next to Samantha, trying to toss something to him. "Wax the rescue board."

Josh opened his hands and Tanner threw the wax at him. Catching it, Josh walked over to where the board was propped up against the tower, opened the lid, and began coating the board, keeping it skid-proof.

Josh looked up at Samantha and found her dazing off. He checked out the direction of her stare and noticed a group of men playing volleyball three or four yards away. "Man, you have got to focus on the job, Sam, or soon your panting tongue will get sunburned."

That snapped Samantha back into reality. "Don't tell me you never check out the guys."

"Yeah, I suppose. But I'm working now. I fight the urge. I'm just petrified while I'm ogling pecs that someone will be drowning."

"Josh!"

"Yeah?" Josh looked back up at Tanner.

"Once you're done waxing, take a can and go out beyond the breakers and make sure you keep people close to shore. There're a few getting too far out."

"Okay." Josh rubbed the board briskly, finishing up.

"You need help getting it to the water?" Samantha asked.

"Yes. Thanks." Josh headed to the hut first to take off his sunglasses and wipe his hands. As he did, he met another permanent who was assigned to their tower on heavily crowded days in the peak season, Angelina. Her gaze lingered on him while she stood at the counter. "What?" Josh paused to confront her.

"I didn't say anything."

At the snotty reply, Josh frowned and kept walking. He met Tanner about to enter the hut.

"How long do you want me out, boss?" Josh asked, rubbing at the lingering wax on his hands.

"Half hour? I don't know. Just keep checking back and I'll wave you in."

"Okay." Josh paused, wishing he could say something else, but what was there to say?

Josh met Samantha who was already leaning the long board against herself.

"Right. Ready?" Josh grabbed a rescue can and put the harness over his chest then he picked up the front of the long board and walked toward the water. The beach was packed, another sunny, hot summer Sunday in the city.

Josh hopped on the board and said, "Thanks, Sam."

"Have fun."

He paddled out beyond the breakers, seeing exactly whom Tanner was referring to. There were three bathers swimming very far from the beach. Straddling the board, Josh dipped his hands into the water, making a smooth path to the swimmers. He glided toward the first one, an older man with a white bathing cap on his head and goggles. "Excuse me! Sir?"

The man appeared startled at the contact. He tread water and spun around.

"Hi. Uh, would you mind moving closer to the shore? You're really too far out."

"Oh, sorry, young man."

"No problem. Thanks." Josh waited as the man swam closer to land.

Leaning over, he paddled to the next swimmer. The same routine followed. The man smiled politely and headed to the beach.

The last swimmer was very far out. Josh was amazed at the guts of some people had that they would go out so deep in the vast ocean. Lying on the board, he accelerated his arm strokes trying to catch up.

As he drew closer, he realized it was an older, heavyset woman, much to his surprise. She too had a bathing cap and dark goggles.

"Ma'am? Ma'am?" She kept swimming. Josh caught back up to her, sliding alongside her. "Hello! Ma'am?"

She heard him and stopped short, grabbing at the long board. Josh held it to steady himself. "Whoa. You okay?"

She looked up at him. "What's wrong?"

"You're way out in deep water. Do you realize that?"

Appearing stunned, she looked back at the beach. "Oh, my God!"

Josh sensed her panic. He began unraveling the rescue can. "Hold this. Let me pull you back in."

"How did I get this far out? I was just daydreaming. Oh, my God!"
"Okay. You're okay. Hold this can. Please."

*~*

Tanner exited the hut and stood behind Angelina who held the binoculars to her eyes. He raised his hand to shield the sun and could see Josh had successfully contacted two out of the three swimmers he had noticed. "What's he doing?"

"He's giving a woman the buoy," Angelina relayed, her eyes still behind the binoculars.

"And? Are they in trouble?" Tanner felt his insides churn.

"I can't tell."

"May I?" Tanner held out his hand.

Angelina gave him the binoculars.

He scanned the horizon and found them. The bather started thrashing suddenly. "Shit." Tanner handed off the binoculars, grabbed a rescue can and took off.

*~*

"Lady, calm down." Josh kept trying to get her to hold the can. "If you calm down and follow my directions I'll get you back to shore. Okay? Hello? Are you listening to me?"

"How did I get out this far? There are sharks in the water!"

Josh took a deep breath and kept trying to keep his balance as she tipped the long board. "What's your name?" She didn't hear him. "Lady! What's your name?"

"Gladys!" she answered, her eyes wild.

"Okay. Gladys. Calm down. Look at me." He waited as she clamored, trying to get on the board with him. "Gladys, just hold this buoy and I will paddle us in. Why can't you follow my instructions?"

She heaved her upper body up and the board dipped down deeply.

"Gladys. Stop. That's not helping either of us." Josh looked up at the shore. It was still a long way off. "Fuck!" Josh gasped as he was flipped off the board as she weighed one side down heavily.

He popped back up and grabbed her, holding her up. "Fine. Grab the board now."

She did, beginning to whimper in panic.

Josh gripped both her and the board and began kicking his feet, getting them to shore. The idea of passing the crowded breakers with the long board seemed daunting. Josh imagined the force of the waves would cause the board to whack someone in the head. There was no way he could control it and Gladys together.

She seemed slightly calmer as they made progress. "Are you okay?" he asked.

"Yes."

"Hang in there." Josh finally caught sight of Tanner swimming toward him with his rescue can in tow.

She screamed and jerked her body.

"What?" Josh asked as she tried to climb on top of him to get away.

"Something brushed my legs!"

"It was probably seaweed. Please calm down." Josh was growing angry with her. He felt like growling, *'What the hell did you swim in the ocean for if you're so fucking paranoid?'*

Tanner closed in on them finally. With a curt professional manner, Tanner pushed his buoy at Gladys. "Hold this."

"No! I'll drown. I have the board."

"The board will be dangerous in the breakers. Hold this!"

Josh loved the way Tanner took control.

"Do it now!" Tanner roared.

She immediately released the board and hugged the buoy.

"Josh, get the board past the breakers."

Watching Tanner guide Gladys to shore, Josh let go a sigh of relief. "Another day in paradise," Josh mumbled as he found his footing, carrying the long board out of the water. "Jesus. Why are people so stupid?"

Josh remembered while he was still in the classroom that the trainers had talked about people panicking. They were right. Josh laid the board down on the sand and stood by, as Tanner made sure the woman was all okay, checking her pulse and some other vitals, doing what he could without his kit.

"Always look back at the beach," Tanner warned her. "The tide will push you out if you let it."

"Yes. I'm sorry." She regained her breath, her goggles shaking in her hand.

"You okay?" Josh asked her.

"I'm fine now. Thank you, young man."

"No problem." Josh smiled at her.

Tanner stood tall and ordered, "Take the board back to the tower."

"Yes, sir!" Josh saluted him.

❧❧

As he watched him go, Tanner wondered what he would do if anything happened to Josh. He must be growing fond of him because the thought of him being harmed made Tanner sick to his stomach.

He spoke a few parting words to the woman, sitting with her to make sure she was all right. Tanner jogged down the beach, catching up to Josh.

"Josh!"

He paused until Tanner fell in beside him.

"Are you all right?"

"Yes. I was just a little unprepared for her panic attack."

"It happens often." Tanner glanced up ahead of them as Josh steered the board around people. "You did great. You kept your composure and brought her in."

"What was I supposed to do with the board if you didn't show up?"

"Push it out beyond the breakers where it can't hit anyone and focus on the victim."

"Yes. Of course. Duh." Josh shook his head.

Tanner was imagining some self-reproach. "Don't."

He caressed Josh's back, and Josh spun his head around to stare at him. Tanner smiled sweetly into his handsome face. "You did very well."

"And? Will I be amply rewarded?" Josh's gleaming green eyes spoke legions.

"If you want, I'll write you up a commendation." Tanner knew that wasn't what Josh meant, but enjoyed teasing him.

"Oh? And?"

"Behave," Tanner whispered.

Giving him an affectionate smile, Josh grabbed Tanner around his waist and held him tight.

Tanner was beginning to like the contact. He draped his arm over Josh's shoulder drawing him closer so they were connected.

"Yum!" Josh wriggled against him.

"Behave." Tanner held up a scolding finger.

Josh snuck a lick of Tanner's arm, smiled shyly and cast his eyes forward toward the tower.

⁓⁓

Tanner could sense Josh waiting for him as he checked out for the day. No matter what he was doing, Josh was never far from his thoughts.

He wondered why.

Was it because he was used to being in a relationship, a marriage, and now, cut loose, he didn't have a new girlfriend to occupy his thoughts?

Before Josh had shown up for his mentorship, Tanner hadn't minded focusing all his attention on the job. It was a diversion.

Was he attracted to Josh?

It was a question he was going round and round with constantly. On some level, the answer was yes. Tanner liked being with Josh, enjoyed speaking to him, was beginning to relish being able to stare at him. But that was it. Or was it?

*Okay, you like Josh touching you or when he puts his arm around your hips, or...*

*Licks you.*

That scared him.

Tanner stepped outside to find Josh indeed lingering on the cement stairs. A little somersault flipped inside his stomach. It was a feeling he used to get in high school. Like the terrible crush he had on his teacher, Miss Fine. And boy was she.

A giddy, lightheaded sensation enveloped Tanner every time he would see her. His skin would tingle, his palms got wet, and his cock would throb.

He was sixteen and infatuated with his science teacher. Now? He was thirty and falling for a twenty-six year old Adonis. *Get a grip on yourself, Tanner. No way can you be gay. Not fucking possible.*

"Hey, stud." Josh gave Tanner a good once over as he approached.

"You need a hobby." Tanner met him, ascending the steps with him.

"I've got one. Gay porn and you."

"Gay porn?" Tanner fished the keys out of his backpack.

"Oops! Did I say that?" Josh gave Tanner a wicked grin.

"So? You've got two days off now and you're going to sit around watching men do it?"

"Never mind. I shouldn't have let that slip. Uh…" Josh peeked around the area first. "You, uh, want to grab a burger or something?"

"I take it that means food and isn't a euphemism for gay sex."

The look on Josh's face was priceless. He let go a roaring laugh, buckling over to hold his belly.

Tanner loved the reaction.

Once he had control over his hilarity, Josh sidled up against Tanner seductively. "Wanna grab my burger?"

"More like a hotdog, I would imagine."

Josh met Tanner's eyes with a very serious expression. "I am beginning to adore you."

The carefree grin fell from Tanner's face at the shock.

"Oops." Josh bit his bottom lip. "Do I talk too much or what? I'm worse than a chick. I'll shut up now."

"My car or yours?" Tanner felt his insides glow. He was beginning to adore Josh as well.

"You drive. You'll be the man of the family." Josh winked at him.

Euphoric suddenly at the idea of them hanging out together, Tanner chirped his alarm on his jeep, opening the door and getting in.

❧❧

Josh was high as a kite at the prospect of spending his time off-duty with Tanner. Sitting on the hot seat, shifting his bottom to wriggle against it, Josh slipped off his flip-flops and brushed his feet against the sand on the floor mats. Josh fastened his seatbelt and smiled at Tanner as he started the jeep and lowered the radio's volume. Josh was completely erect from sitting near Tanner this way, so personal and intimate.

"Where to?" Tanner backed out of the parking space.

"I like everything. Do you have a favorite place?"

Tanner glanced down at their apparel. "I think we're limited."

"Fast food? Pizza? Anything is good."

"Let's hit the drive-through."

"Perfect." Instantly craving contact, Josh reached out to lay his hand on top of Tanner's bare thigh. If they were dating, or if Tanner was gay, he would feel more than comfortable. Undecided, confused as to what he should do, Josh's fingers hovered with indecision.

Tanner noticed it. "Uh…what are you planning on doing with that hand?"

Josh slowly set it down on his own lap and wondered if perhaps this was an exercise in futility. Maybe you couldn't convert straight men like they do in the gay porn films.

They pulled behind a line at Lucy's Drive-Thru.

"Do you like Mexican food?" Tanner removed his wallet from his backpack.

"Yes." Josh rubbed his forehead tiredly.

"You okay?"

"Huh? Yeah fine." *No, I'm not fine. I'm falling madly in love with a man who does not want me.*

When Tanner rested *his* hand on Josh's leg, Josh gasped and spun around to see his face.

"If you're tired, I'll drive you back to your car."

"No. No, Tanner. I'm not tired. I'm…" *Crazy about you.*

Tanner removed his hand to shift gears and pull up to the window. "What do you want?" Tanner asked him.

"Whatever you're getting is fine." Josh couldn't have thought straight at the moment if he wanted to. Josh went for his wallet. Tanner held him back, ordering two enchiladas and lemonades.

Tanner pulled up the emergency brake and seemed to settle back for a long wait.

"Tanner," Josh opened his hands and asked, "are we camping out here?"

"It takes a while. I've learned to be patient." Tanner turned the radio on.

"So…tell me something about yourself." Josh removed his safety belt to be able to pivot in his seat, facing Tanner.

"What do you want to know?"

"I assume you're not married."

"Divorced."

"Oh?"

"Yes. I was married for five years and we split about a year ago."

"Why?"

"She wanted kids. I didn't."

Josh glanced behind them at the growing line. "Didn't she know that before you married her?"

"Yes. But you know women. They think they can change a guy." Tanner met Josh's eyes. "Let me rephrase that…"

Josh smiled. "I know what you mean." He noticed the girl at the window handing them their drinks. Josh thanked Tanner for his, stuffed a straw through the plastic cap of the sweating cup, and drank a slurp. "Was it a bitter break up?"

"Yes. It was. Even though we didn't have children to deal with, it was very emotional." Tanner set his cup in a holder on the console.

"How did she take it?"

"She was very hurt."

Josh imagined losing a guy like Tanner would be brutal. "Were you the one who ended it?"

Tanner lowered his eyes as if the sadness was washing over him. "Let's say it was mutual."

Josh doubted that very much.

Finally their food was handed to them. Tanner placed the bag on the floor by Josh's feet and drove off into the parking lot, hunting for shade.

Tanner backed into a spot and shut off the engine. Josh dug inside the bag for their enchiladas and napkins.

Tanner unhooked his seatbelt and leaned against the driver's door, bending one of his long legs sideways.

Josh had a nice view of Tanner's balls suddenly and wondered how hard it would be to maintain eye contact.

"What about you?" Tanner asked, swallowing his first bite of food.

Josh wiped his lips with a napkin. "Obviously I was never married."

"Obviously." The corners of Tanner's lips curled in a smile.

"Saying that, I just ended a six-month relationship."

"Oh? Why?"

"He cheated on me."

"Ah." Tanner nodded.

Josh said, "I'm the type of guy who wants a loyal relationship. I don't need to be worrying where my partner's dick has been."

"No. I would imagine that would be pretty awful."

"It is with straight couples as well, isn't it?"

"Yup." Tanner licked sauce off his finger.

"Do you have family here in California?"

"No. I came out here on my own once I graduated college and met Anna. Everyone else stayed in Portland."

"Oregon?"

"Yes, Oregon." Tanner finished his enchilada quickly, crushing up the paper it was wrapped in, and picked up his drink. "How about you?"

"All my family is local. They're down in San Diego."

Tanner began stuffing the trash into the bag the food came in.

Josh finished his food, licking his sticky fingers. "That was pretty good for fast food."

"It is decent." Tanner opened the bag for Josh to toss his garbage in.

"Do you have to rush home?"

"No. Why? Do you want to hang out?" Tanner wiped at his fingers with a clean napkin.

"I'm enjoying this." Josh was. Even if he wasn't connected to Tanner's tongue, it was great getting to know him.

"Me too."

"So, do you get hit on by all the chicks at work?"

Tanner smiled shyly. "Some. I used to be married, so being single on the job is a relatively recent development."

"Which girl will you date?" Josh felt his chest burn in jealously, but he needed to know.

"Which girl?"

"Yeah. Samantha? Angelina? Destiny?"

"None of the above."

Josh sat up to stare closely at Tanner's expression, the plastic cup of lemonade in his hand, the straw near his lips. "Why not?"

"Pretty much for the same reason I left Anna. Those women are young and are no doubt hunting for a husband who will father their children."

"How do you know?"

"Come on," Tanner scoffed, dropping his empty cup into the bag as well.

"Don't you at least want to get laid?" Josh was intrigued. He wasn't getting the answers he expected.

"Yeah. Who doesn't? But I can't have sex with one of them. Again, if you were straight, you would know. Women can't just have sex for sex's sake."

"Yes, I have heard that about them." Josh rolled his eyes. "Man, you must think I'm an idiot."

"Far from it."

A flash of fire washed over Josh's body at the look he received. "So? What do you do to get off? Jack off?"

"Pretty much."

Josh cringed and made a face. "What a waste of jizz."

Tanner laughed softly. "Oh? What should I do with it? Donate it to a sperm bank?"

"No!" Josh almost blurted out, *"Let me eat it,"* but thought it sounded slightly repugnant, especially to virgin gay ears.

"You want it?"

At the seductive tone, Josh set his empty cup in the garbage bag and rested his cold, wet hand that had held the iced drink on Tanner's knee. "You have no idea."

"Amazing."

"What's so amazing?" Josh shrugged, running his palm over that hot, hairy knee. "Gay guys like come. Is that a secret?"

"No. I suppose not. I just never saw the world through your eyes."

"I take it you've never had a close male friend who was gay."

"No. Co-workers and acquaintances, yes, but no one close enough to have a conversation like this."

"I feel like a celebrity…" Josh lowered his voice, "or a freak. Which am I to you, Tanner? Some kind of oddity to inspect?"

"What? Shut up. Oddity?" Tanner shook his head in disbelief.

Josh rolled his palm over the ball of Tanner's bent knee. "I can't get over how hot you make me."

"Oh? More than other men you've dated?"

"I hate to admit that." Josh shifted in his seat as his dick pressed against the red fabric of his swimsuit. He lowered his gaze to Tanner's crotch.

Slowly, Tanner concealed it with his hand.

"You think you're blocking the view, but seeing you touch yourself is having the opposite effect, sailor." Josh grinned impishly.

"It seems everything I do turns you on."

"It does. It's torture."

Tanner shifted to face forward in the driver's seat.

Josh's hand dropped to his own lap and he felt completely let down. "Sorry, Tanner."

"Huh? No, don't be. I'm not offended, Josh. I'm just boiling hot. Let me turn the engine on for the air and put the top on."

"Oh!" Relieved, Josh waited as Tanner placed the cloth top back over the roll bars and snapped it in place. Once he was sitting down again, Tanner cranked up the air vents, holding his hand in front of one waiting for it to cool. Tanner rolled up the window.

Josh did the same on his side. Instantly it became more private in their little compartment. "Look," Josh began, "if I overstep my bounds, tell me. The last thing I want to do is upset you, or piss you off. Okay?"

"I will tell you. I'm not the type to not be direct."

"I appreciate that. I suppose I should lay off. I know how it feels to have someone nagging you all the time if you have no interest." Josh thought of Luis.

Tanner's hand found his leg once again, giving it a light squeeze. Josh melted in an instant.

"The irony is, Josh," Tanner whispered softly, "it isn't offensive. I'm not saying I'll be able to fulfill your fantasies, but damn, it's fucking exciting that someone like you is even interested."

Josh felt his heart blow up in his chest he was so stoked. Hope. That gave him hope. "You…you like my little innuendos and flirting?"

A shy smile washed over Tanner's handsome face. "If I say yes, does that instantly make me gay?"

"Christ, don't I wish!" Josh laid his hand over Tanner's, keeping it where it was.

Tanner stared at Josh for a long, wistful moment. "You are pretty damn amazing."

Josh's cock throbbed painfully at his attraction. "So are you, Tanner. You're the best looking fucker I've ever seen." Josh pointed an air vent at himself. "I'm glad this is on because suddenly I'm suffering heatstroke."

"Ditto."

Josh's expression fell as reality set in. His aching heart was telling him to lay off, that he would never get what he wanted from Tanner and he should be content with his friendship. But that's where the pain began. He knew he would never be happy unless he could touch Tanner, passionately, deeply.

"I should get you back to your car." Tanner removed his hand.

Josh missed the heat on his thigh. He straightened up in the seat and clipped the seatbelt back on, trying to stop his heart from breaking.

※※

It was silent on the drive back to the beach. Tanner had a feeling this was killing Josh but didn't know what to do about it. Pulling behind Josh's red convertible, Tanner tried to be jovial. "Okay, buddy, we're here."

Lethargically, Josh opened his safety belt buckle and picked his backpack up off the floor as he slipped his flip-flops on his feet. "Thanks for the meal."

"My pleasure."

Josh stared at him for a few minutes not opening the door to climb out. "Uh, are you busy for our days off? You know, so I can't call you or something?"

"You…you want to call me?" Tanner's skin prickled.

"If that's okay."

"Sure. Why not?" Tanner opened the glove box and removed a pen and a piece of scrap paper. He wrote two numbers down. "Mobile phone, home." He pointed.

"Where do you live?"

"Hawthorne. You?"

"Pasadena."

"That's right." Tanner handed him the paper.

Josh took the pen from his hand and wrote his own info down, including his address, which Tanner had from his paperwork, but didn't stop him. Josh ripped the part of the paper off with his info, giving it and the pen back to Tanner.

"So, I can call you? You won't get mad?"

Tanner smiled. "I won't get mad."

"What…what do you do on your days off?"

Tanner shrugged, putting the jeep in neutral and setting the handbrake. "Not a lot. I suppose since the job is so intense, I turn into a couch potato."

"I understand. You certainly don't need to exercise any more than you already do."

"Exactly. I occasionally read through material to brush up on the medical part. I don't use my paramedic skills often enough and I get rusty."

"You're a paramedic?"

"I am."

"You see, there's so much about you I don't know."

Tanner laughed and roughed up Josh's long shaggy hair.

"I will call you," Josh warned, wagging his finger at him.

"Good."

"Kiss goodbye?" Josh smiled wickedly.

"Cheek?"

"Sold."

Tanner leaned over, giving Josh the side of his face.

Josh lingered, brushing his lips over Tanner's jaw.

The contact made Tanner shiver and close his eyes.

They managed to pull back from each other and were silent. Tanner was shaken by his reaction, trying to control his breathing so it didn't sound like he was panting.

"Wow." Josh cleared his throat. "If I feel like this from pecking you on the cheek, making love to you will kill me."

Tanner wanted to laugh but his insides were twisting from controlling the urge he had to draw Josh to his mouth and suck at his lips.

"Phew, okay, home to take a cold shower or jack off." Josh fumbled with the inside door handle and climbed out.

Tanner almost echoed the sentiment. He had done that exact thing yesterday.

Josh leaned into the jeep. "Right. Bye, hot stuff."

"Bye, Josh." Tanner smiled affectionately at him.

Josh closed the door and waved. Tanner waved back and released the brake, moving out of the lot, looking into his rear view mirror. He watched Josh climb into his car. "Oh man, oh man." Tanner finally could reach into his swimsuit and straighten his hard cock out. The moment he set it upright it pulsated and seeped pre-cum. "I'm insane. Yup, that proves it. I'm completely insane."

# Chapter Seven

Josh lay in bed, staring at the ceiling. The room was lit by the bright sunrise of a Monday morning. While everyone rushed to work, Josh was off. It felt nice.

Josh rolled to his side, crushing the pillow under his head and gazed wistfully at the empty side of the bed. Tanner. Tanner Cameron. Why did he have to meet a man like Tanner?

He yawned, rubbing his scalp through his hair and closed his eyes for a few more minutes of rest. He had no idea what to do today. All his friends would be at work and he was too tired for anything strenuous. It would be a perfect day to lie lazily in Tanner's arms, drowsy and content.

Josh imagined having the balls to actually call him over their days off. *He must think I'm a pest. Some moron who keeps hitting on him and won't take the hint.*

Burrowing under the pillow, Josh hid his head from the light and groaned.

Tanner stretched his back and legs, resisting the urge to get out of bed. He was exhausted. Other than food shopping and laundry, he didn't have anything on his agenda for the two days off.

He reached between his legs to scratch his balls leisurely and had a flash of Josh's face as he sat next to him in his jeep. His cock shifted next to his hand.

Tanner shut his eyes and touched himself lightly. What would it feel like to kiss Josh?

"Oh, fuck no." Tanner sat up and deliberately made an effort to locate an old back issue of Playboy he had stashed somewhere. Rifling through his drawers and closet, he found the dog-eared, year-old magazine he'd bought on a whim. He sat with it on his bed and flipped through it for a photo to get his mind off Josh.

He looked down at his cock and found it limp. In frustration, he rolled the magazine up and whipped it out into the hall.

Tanner rubbed his face in an effort to shed the cobwebs of a rough sleep. His head was beginning to ache. Growling in agony, he fell back against his pillows and closed his eyes.

Josh chewed a piece of toast spread with peanut butter and faintly focused on the room. He felt slightly hung over from all the exertion and heat of the beach. All he wanted was to be a zombie and do nothing.

He sipped his coffee to wash down the peanut butter and looked at the phone. Next to it was the scrap paper Tanner had written his numbers on.

*Call him. Don't call him. Call him. Don't call him.*

He wanted to call but suspected Tanner would be thinking, "Christ, get the hint, fag!"

"Augh!" Josh set the crust of his toast down, stormed across the room, and picked up the phone. He dialed six out of seven numbers and chickened out. Inhaling to find some courage, he once again dialed, forcing himself not to stop until it rang.

"Hello?"

At the sound of Tanner's voice, Josh felt mute.

"Hello?" Tanner asked again.

"Hey. Tanner. It's me." Josh felt like he was the worst pain in the ass.

"Hello, Josh."

"Am…am I bugging you?" His hands grew clammy.

"No. Not at all. I'm just trying to motivate myself to do laundry."

Feeling his legs shake from nerves, Josh sat down on the sofa. "Laundry. That sounds exciting."

"I know. A thrill a minute. What are you up to?"

"Just got up. I stayed in bed all morning. I couldn't force myself out of the cozy blankets."

"I know the feeling. I think the four ten-hour day schedule is so strenuous I spend the two days off recuperating."

Josh's nerves calmed down. They were friends. They should be able to talk to each other.

"Exactly. And I didn't even do a whole week. I'm dreading it."

"You'll get used to it."

Josh bit his lip as silence followed the comment. "You…uh, you doing anything later?"

"What did you have in mind?"

"I don't know. I thought maybe we could just hang out." Josh knew having Tanner alone in one of their homes would be torture. But the urge to be with him was overpowering.

"Hang out and just sit around?"

"Or anything you want to do? I'm easy."

Tanner laughed. "I think I heard that about you."

Josh smiled warmly. "Look, if you're busy…"

"I'm not. Like I said, laundry and food shopping. That's how I'm spending my time off."

Josh felt his pulse rise. "Should I come over to your place or do you want to come here?"

"Whichever you're comfortable with."

"Do you have a house or condo or?"

"A house."

"Oh. Uh, maybe I should come there. My apartment is pretty small. Not much to do here, I'm afraid."

"But watch gay porn?"

Josh replied, "I can't believe I told you that."

"Don't worry about it. I'm teasing you."

"So, what time do you want me to come by?" Josh was growing excited.

"Anytime."

"I…I can be ready within the hour. Is that too soon?" Was he walking on eggshells? It felt like it.

"Sure. Let me give you directions."

Josh hopped up and found a pen and paper. "Shoot." As he wrote down the information, his heart thumped in his chest.

"Do you feel comfortable getting here?"

"Yeah. No problem."

"See you soon."

"See ya." Josh hung up and whooped loudly, pumping his fist in the air. Sprinting to the bathroom, he stripped for the shower and couldn't wait to see Tanner again.

Tanner hung up the phone, allowing the conversation to digest. He wondered what they would do together. He picked up the television guide to see if a ballgame or movie was on that would interest them. Nothing. Tossing the newspaper down, he finished his cup of coffee and set the mug in the sink, washing it. He tidied the house up and headed to the bathroom to shower and shave.

An hour later the doorbell rang. Tanner jumped out of his skin and tried not to sprint to the front door. He had been pacing nervously like this was some kind of date. The idea was absurd.

Tanner ran his hand through his hair nervously and swung the door back.

Josh, his sunglasses on top of his head, wearing a black tank top and beige shorts, looked like a model.

"Hey." Tanner allowed him inside, holding the door for him.

"Hi. Nice house."

"Thanks." Tanner closed the door behind him, peeking down at Josh's brown legs and flip-flop sandals. "Come in. You want something to drink?"

"No. I'm good." Josh paused in the middle of the living room, scanning the area before his attention made its way to Tanner's eyes.

It felt odd to have Josh in his house. Work was one thing. This was private. Knowing Josh was gay and attracted to him made Tanner a mass of nervous anxiety, as if he wouldn't be able to resist his charms and be homosexual by the day's end.

"Wow, this is awkward." Josh folded his arms over his chest. "I had no idea it would be this bad."

Tanner shook himself out of his thoughts and tried to ease through it gracefully. "Nonsense. What's the big deal? We're friends and co-workers, right?"

"Yeah, right." Josh replied.

"Do you want to leave?"

"Fuck no!" Josh stepped closer to him.

Tanner almost moved back in reflex. "This is silly." He tried to laugh it off. "Let's just have a beer on the back patio and relax."

"I'm game."

Tanner passed by Josh, catching a whiff of his enticing cologne as he did. Sensing Josh's gaze on his every move, Tanner took two iced mugs from the freezer. He placed them on the kitchen counter and tipped dark beer into them slowly to avoid a foamy head.

Feeling warmth behind him, Tanner knew Josh was right there. The scent of his aftershave or cologne was so delicious it actually made Tanner's stomach grumble. "Are you behaving behind my back?"

"I'm having wicked fantasies."

"I'll bet." Tanner smiled.

"Can I share them?"

"No!" Tanner laughed in a cough. He pivoted around, pressing against the counter, thinking Josh would be so close to him he'd rub against him. But Josh wasn't as near as he imagined. Tanner handed him one of the beers and gestured to the back sliding door.

Tanner stared at Josh's ass. It was as delightful as any woman's, perfect in the tight fabric of his shorts.

They set their beers down on a round table under an umbrella. The back garden was finely attended with a perimeter of flowering shrubs and a manicured lawn.

"You need a pool." Josh relaxed on a black, wrought iron chair with a padded seat cushion.

"I know. I don't have the cash right now." Tanner sat opposite him, avoiding the chance of contact.

"Did the divorce break you?" Josh sipped his beer, placing his sunglasses on his nose.

"No. She didn't go for the jugular. I have no alimony payments either. She got the house though. I had to get a huge loan to buy this one."

"Bummer."

Tanner shrugged, gulping the beer. "I manage."

"Did you get your laundry done?" Josh stuck his tongue in his cheek as if he were teasing.

"Some. I have to remember to put a load in the dryer."

"I'd like to put a load somewhere."

Tanner met his wicked smile. "Man, are you bad!"

"I'm horny. I suppose I have a very high sex drive."

"So do I but I do try and rein it in a little."

"Do you?"

"Do I what?" Tanner wiped the foam off his lip.

"Have a high sex drive?"

"I suppose. Don't most men?"

"Yes. I think that's part of the attraction to gay life. Men like to do it, a lot."

"True."

"I knew I'd be dealing with a hard-on all day sitting near you." Josh slid his sunglasses back on top of his head, as if he couldn't decide where to put them.

Tanner choked on his beer as he tried to swallow.

"Shit. Just tell me to shut up." Josh's cheeks went crimson.

Coughing to clear his windpipe, Tanner was suddenly dealing with an erection as well and couldn't imagine acting on it with Josh. It just seemed surreal. Tanner looked across the table at Josh's luminous eyes. They made Tanner's skin prickle. There was something to Josh's gaze. Something deeper than friendship. An odd sensation washed over Tanner. Was Josh falling in love with him?

Josh was in agony. The man of his dreams was a few inches from him and may as well have been three thousand miles away. He was completely unattainable.

This was a first for Josh. He'd managed to find someone to have sex with his whole adult life. This was the worst scenario he could imagine. Why the hell did he come here? It was making him miserable.

"Josh?"

"Hm?"

"Are you okay?"

Josh didn't know what to say. Tanner appeared very concerned. This was their day off and they shouldn't be moping and upset. "Yes. I'm fine. So, uh... what music do you like to listen to?"

Tanner set his mug down. "All kinds. I have diverse tastes."

Nodding, Josh took another gulp of beer. He wished it was hard liquor so he could get inebriated. "Do you read?"

"I used to read fiction. Lately, I've been keeping up on job related topics. Mostly the medical field, especially for first responders, is constantly being updated."

"Right. Paramedic." Josh was incredibly impressed with Tanner.

"Yes."

"Did you do that before you became a lifeguard?"

"I originally wanted to be a firefighter."

Josh's dick went wild, pulsating in his shorts. As discreetly as he could, he slipped his hand in to move it upright to get it comfortable. "A fireman?"

"Yes. But Anna had a fit. So I diverted toward the lifeguard service."

"Do you know scuba?"

"Yes. All the permanents have to know it."

"I'd like to take that course. I'm really looking forward to the training."

"Did you sign up?"

"No. But I will soon."

"Yes. You should get that done."

Josh had an image of them spending training time together. There were many extras to learn on the job, including recertification of all the skills. They were bound to overlap. "I am so glad I was assigned to you, Tanner."

"Me too. I feel like I can depend on you for any situation. And since you're brand new, that's really impressive."

That perked Josh up. "Really?"

"Really." Tanner finished his beer and reclined back against the seat.

"Am I even more impressive than the permanent women?"

Tanner looked aside for a minute, leaned his elbows on the table and spoke in a low confidential tone, "Look, I'm not supposed to encourage sexism."

"But?" Josh was intrigued.

"But…I feel nervous asking the women to do certain tasks. I know they're capable, don't get me wrong. They had the same training as we did. I just feel if they got hurt I'd be devastated."

Under the table's cover, Josh rubbed his stiff cock through his shorts. "I understand."

"Good. I knew you would."

"What about the past students you've mentored? Any stand outs?"

"They were pretty good, but not nearly as good as you."

Josh was going completely mad. The urge to flip out his dick and jerk off was overwhelming. He could not calm down. "You…you think I'm that good?"

"Are you kidding me? I wouldn't send a newbie out alone on the long board during their first days of mentorship."

"Really?" Josh slipped his hand partway into the front of his shorts. The tips of his fingers got sticky from his oozing cock.

"Yes. I trust you. Your confidence and skill level far exceeds anyone else I've encountered."

"I had no idea." Josh wiped at his sticky slit with his thumb.

"I suppose I should say these things to you while we're on duty to let you know what I think. I just don't want it getting around that I think you're better than anyone else I've mentored. I may hurt some feelings."

"Some guards do have big egos." Josh kept swiping at the steady stream of pre-cum that was pulsing out of his dick.

"No kidding. Christ, the women are so much worse than the guys in that respect. They strut around pretending to be Pamela Anderson."

That made Josh laugh. "Is that why you keep your distance from them?"

"Yes. I told you why the other day."

"I remember. Kids." His hand was getting covered. He couldn't wipe it on his pants because it would show on the beige material.

"Yup. Kids." Tanner sighed heavily. "I don't know why I don't want them. I just don't. They're like little bloodsuckers. My sister has two and they drive me crazy. The diapers? The screaming? The tantrums? You have to be insane."

"I agree. I have no interest whatsoever." Josh tried to wipe his fingers on the tale of his shirt. The amount he was dripping was ridiculous.

"No? Don't want to be a father?"

"Other than the obvious logistical problem with that, no, I have no desire to go through the trauma of rearing a little brat."

"Huh."

"Huh?" His stomach was now as sticky as his fingers.

"It just never occurred to me..."

"What?" Josh leaned closer. "That that would be yet another advantage to a gay affair?"

Tanner replied, "Well, yes."

The mess was getting totally out of control. "Tanner, where's your bathroom?"

"I'll show you." He stood and opened the slider.

Josh took his hand out of his shorts and made sure his shirt was untucked to hide the little disaster.

"Right here," Tanner said as he turned on a light for him.

"Thanks."

"You got yourself into a state, didn't you?" Tanner glanced downward.

Stunned that he was nailed, Josh didn't know what to say. Finally he just laughed it off. "I'm a sticky mess. I'm ashamed of myself."

"Do I really turn you on that much?"

Swallowing his intimidation, Josh slowly raised the bottom of his shirt to reveal what he was hiding. "I'm in agony, Tanner."

"Holy shit."

Josh peered down at himself. The blushing tip of his cock was showing and the drying cum all over his shirt and skin was humiliating.

"Wow."

Josh quickly looked at his expression. Tanner appeared lost as he gazed at his body. He started to pant in response. "I can't control myself around you. It was a bad idea to come here. Literally." Josh tried to laugh but he felt like crying.

"I'll let you clean up." Tanner turned his gaze aside.

"Yes. Thanks." Josh bit his lip at his emotions and closed the bathroom door, leaning his forehead against it. Josh battled back his frustration.

---

Tanner took a few shaky steps from the bathroom and paused. The sight of Josh's cock head sticking out of the top of his beige shorts, and the creamy pre-cum matting Josh's soft hair on his belly caused chills to race over Tanner's skin. He'd never observed another man's hard, oozing cock in his life.

Using the wall to steady himself, Tanner made it to the kitchen and leaned both hands on the counter to think. His own dick was going berserk, throbbing in its bent position. The idea that he turned Josh on to that extent was more than flattering, it was tormenting. "I knew it was a bad idea having him here." Tanner ground his jaw and had no idea what to do. Should he ask Josh to leave? Or were they supposed to pretend that didn't happen? Was Josh jacking off in his bathroom?

The thought of Josh working his shaft and coming made chills flash all over his skin.

*Stop! Stop thinking about him in that way! I am not gay!*

The bathroom door opened, causing Tanner to jolt in fear. It was too quick. Tanner didn't think Josh pleasured himself that fast. Could he?

"Maybe I should go."

Tanner twisted around on his heels to face him. The look of devastation on Josh was painful. "You don't have to leave. I thought maybe we could order a pizza for dinner."

Josh dabbed at the corner of his eye. "You think I should stay?"

"Why not?" Tanner didn't want him to go.

Josh replied, "Because I didn't bring a change of clothing."

Tanner closed the gap between them and touched Josh's cheek lightly. "Though I know this must be embarrassing for you, I find it endearing, not offensive."

Josh trapped Tanner's hand in both of his and used it to continue to caress his cheek.

"Josh, this must be so hard on you."

"It is. It's murder. But I never want to do anything to lose you as a friend. So please don't let that happen."

"I won't. Promise."

Josh kissed Tanner's knuckles lightly. Though Tanner knew he should draw back from the touch, it was mesmerizing to watch Josh's lips and see his soft, tender side.

∽∾

In the bathroom, Josh had cleaned up and splashed his face, resigned to leave and put some distance between them. But Tanner invited him to stay. Josh felt relief. He kept imagining Tanner getting so revolted by him he'd kick him out and shun him. But that wasn't happening.

Tanner's large hand was limp and pliable. Josh ran the back of it against his cheek, over his lips gently, and tasted it with his tongue. Unable to resist, he drew one finger into his mouth to suck, running his tongue along the length of it, pulling deep suction against it. Josh spun into a fantasy. He kept waiting for Tanner to jerk his hand back in disgust, but he didn't. Slowly opening his eyes, Josh found Tanner's astonished gape as he focused on Josh's mouth.

Josh watched Tanner's expression as he shifted fingers, sucking the middle one. It appeared Tanner was too stunned to believe what he was seeing.

Josh dragged his teeth along Tanner's skin. His cock was once again hard and oozing. This man made him completely nuts.

"Josh."

At the urgency of his name, Josh allowed Tanner's finger to slip slowly out of his lips.

"M…maybe y…you sh…should g…go…" Tanner sputtered, shaking visibly.

"I'm so sorry." Josh found Tanner pale and sweating profusely. "Oh God…" Josh moved away from him, running for the door. Once he was outside in the heat, Josh staggered his way to his car and dug the key out of his pocket. "I'm an idiot! I'm such a fucking idiot!"

Swiping at the tears falling from his eyes, Josh knew if he kept pushing Tanner to do what he could not do, he would surely shove him out of his life totally.

The sun beating down on him from above, Josh drove to Luis' townhouse out of desperation. *If I get back with Luis, I will have to stop thinking about Tanner.*

Just as he was pulling up to Luis' address, Josh hit the brakes. Luis was laughing, walking with another man on his driveway where a strange car was parked. Swerving to get away, Josh pumped the gas pedal and raced down the street, assuming Luis had seen him. How many red convertibles drove down his side street a day?

Not wanting to go home, Josh headed to the beach and finally found a spot by a meter. Pausing before he climbed out, he shut off the engine and felt like he owed Tanner a huge apology. "Leave the guy alone!" he screamed, causing heads to turn.

Covering his face in shame, Josh battled to hold back his tears.

*≈≈*

Tanner felt like passing out. Watching Josh give his fingers head, feeling the velvety softness of his mouth, knowing Josh was most likely creaming his shorts again, Tanner didn't think he could keep resisting this temptation. It was maddening.

He tripped over his bare feet to his bedroom. Tanner opened his zipper and stripped down his shorts. His cock protruded from his briefs and dripped precum profusely. "Jesus Christ!" Tanner fell backward onto his bed and jacked off vigorously. He came so hard it sprayed him under his jaw and coated his shirt. Lying still, Tanner recuperated before he found the strength to wash up. Tanner moved slowly, heading to the bathroom.

He felt terrible for Josh.

Tanner picked up his phone and dialed Josh's mobile number first, then his home. No answer. He left a message. "Josh, it's me. Look, I don't want you to beat yourself up for what happened. It's okay." Pausing, trying to think and dreading the self-flagellation Josh would inflict upon himself, Tanner added, "Don't torture yourself about it. Today did nothing to jeopardize your job or our friendship. Please. Don't worry." He hung up and wrung his hands. If anything happened to Josh, he'd never forgive himself.

# Chapter Eight

Wednesday morning Josh got ready for work. His red bathing suit was washed and fit snuggly on his hips. He slipped a white t-shirt on and found his keys and flip-flops. The message from Tanner on Monday did offer comfort. At least he wasn't labeled a pervert and ejected from the job. But Josh warned himself to lay off the man. There was nothing worse than unwanted sexual attention. He knew that better than most.

His mood was foul. The last two nights of shut-eye sucked. All he did on his second day off was sleep on and off all day, barely eating.

Maybe seeing Luis moving on with his life hurt him. Was that the same guy Luis had the affair with? Josh didn't know and tried not to care. But at the moment, in his fragile state, everything felt like a jab to his ego.

Josh parked his car, seeing the white jeep already there. Josh waited while his roof flipped closed over his head, anticipating a chance of rain sometime during the day. Head down, he scuffed his flip-flops to the beach, wishing he could crawl back in bed and hide.

∽∽

Tanner noticed Josh the minute he walked into the room to check his assignments. Seeing Josh appear so defeated upset Tanner horribly.

His captain asked him, "Is that the recruit you were talking about?"

"Yes." Tanner glanced back at his captain.

"You want him as a permanent on your tower?"

"Please. He's got a fantastic grasp on the job and that area of the beach is manic during the summer."

"You don't usually make personal requests to retain your students, Tanner. I'm surprised."

"This one's exceptional. I'd hate to lose him."

"Okay. I'll defer to your judgment. Just tell him today he'll be assigned to work with you."

"Thanks, Captain."

Tanner left the building looking for Josh who had disappeared. Spotting him standing with Destiny, Tanner approached them. "Hey."

"Hi, Tanner." Destiny replied. "I was waiting for Nathan and Joe. Do you want us all to walk together?"

Even though Tanner wanted to talk to Josh alone, he knew once they were at their tower they'd have a chance. "Sure." Josh wouldn't meet his eyes. Tanner wondered if he was being forward in getting Josh assigned to him without asking him first.

Joe and Nathan showed up.

Tanner and Josh walked together in front of them. Destiny dove into some idle chitchat with Tanner, which he just wasn't in the mood for.

"It was a great movie, Tanner. One of those romances, you know, where the guy sweeps the girl off her feet?" She didn't seem to mind or care if Tanner was even paying attention. "I just love movies like that. You sure you wouldn't want to go?"

"What?" He barely made eye contact with her he was so preoccupied. "Go where?"

"Never mind!" she huffed.

They arrived at their tower. Josh seemed as if he wanted to hide, rushing to get away from him. Tanner felt like complete shit.

"See you guys later," Joe and Nat said, walking to the next tower with Destiny.

Tanner entered the hut and checked his first aid kit to make sure it was complete before he did anything else.

He finally stepped out to the rail, looking for Josh. Josh was standing near the water's edge holding a rescue buoy.

Tanner wondered if Josh would avoid conversation with him from now on. The experience over their days off must have been devastating. It was rejection of the worst kind. Waves of anxiety over the pain he was inflicting on such a kind man tortured him.

He felt like he shouldn't push Josh if he was uncomfortable. So Tanner left him on his own for a while. A rescue can in his hand, Tanner took off in the opposite direction to exercise. The morning breeze cleared his mind. Clouds formed low on the horizon and the forecast called for a chance of rain. Tanner expected a light crowd for a weekday with the threat of showers looming.

He kept ruminating over what had happened between him and Josh. The sight of Josh's engorged dick head sticking up from his shorts, all that creamy cum staining his lower abdomen and black shirt, not to mention Josh sucking on his fingers... It was driving him to distraction.

He'd satisfied himself three times over that incident in a twenty-four hour period. It was as if he couldn't stop the excitement he felt about it.

"I've gone completely off the deep end. I need to get fucking laid. By a woman," he emphasized. But he didn't want a woman now. How sick was that?

Should he just ask ditzy Destiny on a date to get Josh out of his system? Thinking about the nightmare scenario of using Destiny that way, Tanner had no interest in Destiny. It would only cause hurt feelings

"Josh, what have you done to me?" Tanner felt exhausted from two bad nights of sleep in a row, tossing and turning. Tanner hadn't been able to stop thinking about Josh's mouth, the expression on Josh's face when he sucked on his fingers, and the urge to allow Josh to go down on him. It was painful it was so compelling.

Tanner spun around in the sand, running over his wet tracks. He could barely make out Josh heading toward him possibly over a mile away. The beach was vacant due to the early hour and the weather prediction. Luckily, it seemed as if it was going to be a slow day.

Catching his breath as he stopped in front of their tower, tossing the can aside, Tanner dropped down to do push-ups, feeling spent from crappy days off.

∽∾

As he drew near, Josh could see Tanner doing some exercises on the damp sand. Josh felt like holding up and going in a different direction. It was crazy. Tanner was his mentor for one last day and he needed to stay with him.

Josh met up with Tanner, tossed the can he was holding and stared at him. He waited, gazing at Tanner as he finished his repetitions and sat back on his heels. Josh felt stupid and adolescent. He wanted to run away.

"Josh?" Tanner met his eyes.

Josh's insides lit on fire. He took a step backward.

"What's wrong?" Tanner's deep voice sent chills all over Josh's body. "Do your workout."

It was an order. A cold order. Josh fell to his knees on the sand. Without releasing the gaze of Tanner's sky blue eyes, Josh positioned himself for pushups and pumped them like a machine. Up and down, he kept pushing his body until the ache was tearing at his muscles, continuing through the agony. Josh didn't care if it hurt. He didn't care about anything.

∽∾

Tanner knew Josh was in pain. He read it on his face very clearly. And the ache wasn't only from his strenuous exercise, it was from what he believed was rejection.

Finally Josh's body gave out. The last few reps he pushed made his arms shake.

Tanner was suffering watching him punish himself that way. "Enough."

Josh sneered and did two more, resting in the upright position.

"Don't strain yourself. You need to be able to perform if needed," Tanner scolded.

Another curl of his lip and Josh did two more. The muscles of Josh's arms and torso were ripped. Not an ounce of fat showed through his bronze skin.

Tanner couldn't take the torture Josh was inflicting on himself. He pushed Josh over, forcing him to stop the self-imposed discipline.

"Josh, we need to talk." Tanner stood, brushing off the sand from his knees, gesturing to the tower.

Josh glared at Tanner from under his thick brown hair. Tanner felt the effect of those light eyes and tried not to flinch at the sexual potency.

Tanner picked up the rescue can, pausing so Josh was walking in front of him. Tanner had the urge to brush away all the sand sticking to Josh's sweaty skin. It seemed as if Josh was so deep inside himself, he didn't even realize he was coated in it.

They hung up the buoys on the rail and Josh entered the hut. Tanner closed the door for privacy. It was dim in the interior, but Tanner did not turn on a light. "What's going on?"

"Nothing." Josh's jaw muscles twitched.

Unable to resist the impulse, Tanner moved closer to Josh, beginning to brush away the sand from his skin. "I need you to be focused while you're at work, Joshua." He swept the sand off Josh's back, his side, working down his hip to his legs. "I can't have this attitude. You need to lighten up."

Tanner cleared most of the grains from Josh's hot skin, stood tall, and looked at him. Josh's eyes were closed and his posture was stiff as a rod. And so was the cock under his bathing suit.

"Josh. Look at me." Tanner's frustration at seeing Josh's torment of the flesh, made his heart ache.

Slowly, in the dimness, Josh's long dark eyelashes fluttered open. Tears filled his eyes.

"Come here." Tanner felt a lump in his throat and reached out to him. At Josh's reluctance, Tanner gripped Josh's shoulders and impelled him into an embrace. At the crush of Josh's body against his, Tanner felt so much pleasure his own eyes burned. "Stop punishing yourself. For Christ's sake, Josh. Stop it." Tanner felt Josh's body shudder and heard a sob break his throat.

"I can't touch you."

Tanner rubbed Josh's back in comfort. "Yes, you can."

"No. It kills me." Josh arched back, pressing his hands against Tanner's chest.

"I need you to calm down." Tanner could feel Josh's cock as it throbbed against his. It sent a wash of tingles down Tanner's back. "I need you to inhale deeply and release this anger you're holding. Josh, this job is too dangerous to be preoccupied."

Suddenly Josh's body went limp and all his weight shifted to Tanner.

"Better. Now stop fretting over this."

"I slept like crap the last two nights, Tanner."

"Me too."

Josh leaned back to see his face.

"Yes." Tanner nodded.

"Why?"

"I don't know." Tanner did, but damned if he was going to tell him. He released Josh and dabbed at Josh's damp cheeks. "Just stare at the waves and unwind. Okay?"

"Yeah. Sorry, Tanner." Josh rubbed his face.

"Take a minute to compose yourself."

"Okay. Thanks."

"No problem." Tanner took a step back, staring at Josh's silhouetted body against the back lighting from the Plexiglas windows. He was absolutely fucking incredible. Tanner forced his eyes away and left the hut, closing the door behind him.

Destiny approached their tower. "Is everything okay, Tanner? Nat and I noticed the tower was vacant."

"Huh? No, everything is fine."

"Is Josh's training going all right?"

"Yes. He's just a little distracted today."

"Well, he picked a good day for it. It's dead." Destiny nodded to the empty beach.

"True. My guess is it'll rain and, we'll be counting the minutes to go home."

"You never know," Destiny said, "it may suddenly clear up."

"Maybe."

"Okay, Tanner. I just wanted to make sure you guys were all right."

"Thanks, Destiny. I appreciate it."

"No problem. Where's Josh assigned to next?"

Tanner bit his lip on his reply. Before he did, he heard the door of the hut and looked back. Josh drew near, his head down. Without giving away that he had requested Josh to be "his", Tanner said, "See ya later, Destiny."

She got the hint and walked off.

Josh met him at the rail. Tanner pressed his hand against the nape of Josh's neck under his long shaggy hair. "You okay?"

"Yes. I am." Josh met his eyes boldly.

"Good." Tanner smiled sweetly at him. He wanted to tell him they were going to work together. He just didn't know when.

༄༅

By mid-afternoon, the sun came out and some surfers emerged with it. The windy day caused the waves to be churning with foamy white caps and strong undercurrents.

Josh took off his t-shirt in the heat and looked down at his chest. It was glistening from sunscreen mixed with his sweat. He draped his shirt over the rail and watched colorful surfboards appear and dip between sets of waves.

"Do you surf, Josh?" Tanner asked.

"No. Never had the impulse."

"I did it once. I wasn't very good at it. Why don't you grab a can and go walk the beach."

*Fuck you.* Josh snarled, reached over the rail, and took a rescue buoy. Without looking back, he started his stroll down at the water's edge as more and more bathers appeared under the clearing sunny sky.

Since the water was so turbulent, Josh took special care to keep his eyes peeled. As he passed the swimming zone into the surfing area, marked by a yellow and black checkered flag, Josh paused to watch the young people trying to catch that elusive wave.

"Josh!"

He spun around to see Nathan catching up, a can in his hand.

"What are you doing so far down the beach?"

"I'm bored and I think Destiny and Joe are sick of talking to me. They sent me off on my own." They began walking across the wet sand together. "Do you know where your assignment is tomorrow?"

"What?" Josh tilted to look at him. "Oh. No. I didn't even think to look."

"I'm right at that tower." Nathan pointed a few yards down the beach.

A dark sense of dread washed through Josh. *Most likely I'll be banished from Santa Monica. Probably to Catalina Island.*

"I wouldn't surf in this. It's too rough." Nathan paused in his tracks.

Josh counted over a dozen boards in various positions in the water. "I suppose the rougher it is, the better the wave."

"I guess. I'm just a chicken shit."

"Me too, Nat. No way would I be tempted to surf in water that choppy." Josh gave a quick look behind them. Very few people were in the water swimming. Most were standing in the shallows, cooling off.

They continued heading down the beach. Josh could feel the temperature climbing now that the clouds were gone.

A yellow and blue surfboard popped straight up in the air through the water. It startled both Josh and Nathan at its abrupt action. Instinctively, they paused to wait for the young man attached to it by a lead, to surface.

"Uh oh," Nathan sighed.

"I don't see him yet. Do you?" Josh began to unravel his rescue buoy. A quick flash of skin appeared through the next wave. "Shit!" Josh took off running, placing the harness over his chest. Spearing the wave, he dove under the breakers and searched for the young man.

Popping up, he caught his breath and could see he was nearing the empty surfboard.

"Follow the lead!" Nathan shouted, swimming closer.

Dunking under again, Josh found where the nylon rope attached to the board and tracked it to the end. He felt a leg. Grabbing the young man around his waist, Josh rocketed through the water with a strong bound off the sand and brought the surfer up. "He's out! Get Tanner! He needs medical help. I'll get him to shore and start CPR."

"You sure? I can help get him to shore."

"No! Go!" Josh held the limp surfer around his chest, swimming him closer to the beach. He tried to sense if the man's ribs were expanding and didn't feel a thing under his forearm. Seeing Nathan swimming to shore frantically and then signaling with his buoy as he ran, Josh felt the young man jerk in his arms and looked at his face. His eyes were wide open and he was choking out salt water.

"Thank fuck!" Josh squeezed him tight to let him know he was with him and continued bringing him to dry land.

ಲ‍ಲ

Destiny shouted as she ran to Tanner's tower, "Tanner! Nathan's giving the distress signal and Joe's out on another rescue!"

Tanner spun around, grabbed his first aid kit out of the hut and rushed out.

They intercepted Nathan on the beach. Nathan gasped for air. "A surfer needs help, Tanner."

Tanner sprinted with his kit in his hand as Destiny and Nathan struggled to keep up.

Tanner gasped at the sight. Two men were down, one was Josh. His skin went ice cold. His heart in his throat, Tanner doubled his efforts to get there.

The surfer was lying on his back choking up saline and vomiting, but Josh was on his face on the wet sand, the surfboard brushing up against his body with the shifting water. Passing the surfer by, Tanner grabbed Josh and dragged him out of the water's edge. He shoved the surfboard onto the sand preventing it from hitting him and had a feeling Josh had been knocked out by it as he brought the young man to shore.

Tanner found Destiny and Nathan crouched down by the surfer, rolling him to his side to make sure he didn't choke on his vomit.

Glad she and Nathan had the surfer's first aid in hand, Tanner located Josh's pulse. Tanner's stomach cramped with anxiety until he felt it beating under his finger with relief. Next he checked his breathing. It was very shallow but at least he was breathing. Looking over his shoulder, seeing Destiny talking with the surfer, Tanner knew the guy was okay and turned all his attention on his co-worker, a man he adored.

"Okay, baby." Tanner coaxed, running his hands over Josh's head, checking for injury. "You're okay...wake up." He used his fingers to run down his neck, his shoulders, his back, arms, pelvis, and his legs. Opening his kit, he pulled out a C-collar and wrapped it around Josh's neck in case he had a neck or spine injury.

As he did, it felt as if Josh's breathing halted.

"Oh, God..."

Destiny appeared by his side. "How's he doing?"

"I think I lost his respiration. Signal to the next tower we need help."

She bolted upright and used the rescue buoy to attract the attention of the lifeguard at the next tower.

Tanner crouched down, pressing his lips against Josh's. Just as he was about to blow air forcefully, he felt some enter his mouth. The relief he experienced was great. Taking a moment to be sure, instead of turning his cheek to feel the air, Tanner closed his eyes and brushed Josh's lips against his own again. His breathing puffed against Tanner's mouth. "Josh, if you were awake right now you'd be loving this." Tanner was, but had to keep his wits about him.

Josh's eyes opened.

Tanner pulled back to see his face. A hand in his hair held him firm.

"Kiss me again."

"Joshua, are you hurt? Don't kid around."

Josh reached up to the plastic collar. "Am I hurt?" Josh asked in confusion.

"I think the surfboard hit you." Tanner was so thankful Josh was all right, he felt like bursting.

"Take this thing off."

"No. Not until we're sure you don't have any neck or back injuries."

Josh made a move to sit up. "Where's the surfer?"

"He's behind you. Josh, stop moving."

"I'm okay." Josh yanked at the collar, peeling the Velcro off.

"Stop moving!" Tanner gripped his arms.

"I don't hurt anywhere, Tanner. If I was badly hurt I would feel it."

"Wiggle your toes." Tanner watched as he did. "Move your fingers."

"Get this horrible thing off me." Josh wrenched out of the collar and found Destiny staring at him while she was comforting the young man.

"You are a stubborn mother fucker," Tanner scolded. "What did they teach you about possible spine injuries?"

"I'm okay. See?" Josh waved his hands and bent his legs. "Ow." He touched his hip, yanking down his suit. Josh exposed a bruise, bright red and turning purple. "I think I found my injury."

Tanner knelt on the sand and ran his hand over the spot.

"Yes, it's much better now," Josh teased.

Nathan finally made his way over, gasping from his run. "Josh, are you okay?"

"Yeah. I think so." He reached up for Nathan to help him stand.

"Josh!" Tanner admonished. "What are you doing? Sit down until the medics arrive."

"You're a paramedic, Tanner. And you're all I need." Josh's eyes lit up. "Get me upright, Nat."

Tanner rubbed his face in frustration and stood, holding Josh's right side while Nathan held his left. Once Josh was up, Tanner ran his hands up and down his legs again, making sure he was okay.

"You're turning me on." Josh laughed.

Nathan broke up with hilarity and doubled over.

"Christ, Josh," Tanner chided, "You are incorrigible." He noticed Destiny was observing the entire time.

Josh walked over to the surfer on unsteady feet. "You okay, man?"

"Yeah. Just my ankle is sprained. Thanks, dude." He reached out his hand. Josh shook it. He asked Destiny, "Are you getting him a ride to the hospital?"

"Yes. We were going to send you both."

A rescue truck finally made its way toward them.

"I'm fine." Josh rubbed his hip.

Tanner tucked the C-collar back in his kit and met with the two paramedics.

Destiny informed the medics, "The surfer was vomiting and appears to have a sprained ankle. I assume he swallowed a ton of water, and Josh—"

"I'm okay, Destiny. I'm not going to the hospital."

"Joshua." Tanner shook his head at him.

"My mother calls me that," Josh laughed, "and you don't look anything like her, believe me."

Tanner caught a strange expression of suspicion on Destiny's face. It made him feel slightly dizzy in its accusatory glare.

The medics helped the surfer get into the truck. Once he was seated in the rig, one of the men approached Josh.

"Get over here and sit your ass on the running board," the medic ordered.

Tanner escorted Josh to the truck, sitting him down. He knew the paramedics from his many years in the business. They were both firefighters. Hunter Rasmussen and Blake Hughes. He had a feeling once Josh got over his stubbornness and got a good look at the two handsome men, he'd react with his usual sly wit.

Standing behind Hunter, crossing his arms over his chest, Tanner noticed Nathan and Destiny still lingering. "You two can head back to your tower. Thanks for your help."

"Should I take your kit back, Tanner?" Nathan offered.

"Yes. Thank you, Nat." Tanner said to Destiny, "Leave one can, take the other."

"Okay, Tanner." She shot him a suspicious glare and walked off with Nathan.

Tanner ignored it, focusing his attention back on Josh.

Hunter was shining a light into his brilliant green eyes.

"Are you guys firemen?" Josh asked, smirking.

"Yup." Hunter shut off the light and ran his hands over Josh's head, checking his scalp.

"Oh, yes…" Josh closed his eyes. "I love firemen."

Tanner covered his laugh. Blake spun around to exchange looks with him. Tanner shrugged innocently.

"Find 'em hot, leave 'em wet," Josh moaned.

"Josh, behave." Tanner bit his lip to stop laughing.

Blake smiled. "He's well enough to flirt."

"I'm fine. But don't stop touching me." Josh spread his legs. "I think I hit my balls on the sand."

Hunter met Tanner's eyes. "Is he your responsibility, Tanner?"

"Unfortunately."

"He's a real handful."

"More than a handful," Josh purred, "especially with two gorgeous firemen groping my body."

"Groping?" Hunter paused in his exam. "I'm checking you for injuries. Not groping."

"Damn. I swear my ass and nuts are really sore."

"Mr. Elliot. Rein it in a little." Tanner continued to hold back his roar of laughter.

"Sorry, Tanner." Josh winked. "You're the one who insisted I get…felt up."

"He's just fine." Hunter stood, snapping off his rubber gloves. "We need to get our surfer friend here to the hospital."

"Dude!" the young surfer yelled. "Hold my board. I'll call a friend to pick it up."

"Okay." Josh stood off the running board of the truck slowly.

Hunter and Blake shook Tanner's hand. "Good to see you again, Tanner."

"You, too. Take care of yourselves."

Josh stood next to Tanner, waving as they left. "What is it about firefighters, Tanner? I get all weak in the knees."

Tanner stared down at Josh. "You should go home and rest."

Josh checked his watch. "Only an hour to go. I can make it."

Josh went to retrieve the surfboard, but Tanner stopped him. "Let me. Will you chill?"

"Don't treat me like an invalid."

"You were out cold." Tanner picked up the board and balanced it in one hand, resting it against his side under his arm.

"I was not."

"Yes, you were."

"Are you sure?"

"Why do you think I was about to give you mouth-to-mouth?"

"'Cause you wanted to see what it was like to kiss me?" Josh blinked his lashes flirtatiously and picked up the remaining rescue buoy.

"No. Because I thought you weren't breathing." Tanner started walking Josh back to the tower. "Are you okay? Tell me the truth, Josh."

"I feel a little rough. Okay? But I'm not hurt. Other than my pride and a bruise on my hip."

"That board must have clobbered you."

"I think it whacked me across my back. I remember feeling the wind knocked out of me."

"Ah. Okay." Tanner wrapped his free arm around Josh's shoulder. "I was really worried about you."

"Thanks, Tanner." Josh slung his arm around Tanner's hips.

They walked in silence for a while. Tanner was haunted by the sensation of kissing Josh. He knew he would be the minute he did it. But he had to. It was a professional decision not a sexual one. Well, maybe both.

Josh slid his hand to Tanner's bottom, pressing his palm over one of Tanner's cheeks as they walked.

"You're trouble," Tanner warned.

"I love how strong you are. I can feel your powerful, masculine strength with each of your steps. It just pulsates through you."

Tanner smiled at the delightful compliment. As they moved down the sparse beach, Tanner felt Josh's finger tracing the crack between his cheeks. Tanner twisted to look back to see if anyone was watching. He didn't want Josh to have to stop it felt so nice.

"Do you have any idea how delicious you are?" Josh purred.

"I'm just relieved you feel well enough to molest me."

"I'm just relieved you're allowing it."

Tanner knew once they drew closer to their tower, which was in view from Destiny and Nathan's, Josh would have to quit doing it. Josh added a little more pressure, pushing his suit into his crack. Tanner tensed up, getting an erection from the thrill rushing over him. "Josh, that's enough."

Josh slipped his hand into Tanner's bathing suit. Tanner stopped moving and gasped. "What are you doing?"

"Getting the material out of your butt. There." He flipped his hand out of the waistband.

The shocks of delight reverberated around Tanner's body like a ricocheting bullet. Tanner dug his nails into the surfboard he was holding and squeezed Josh's shoulder.

Josh spun around to see his expression. "Oh, yes."

Tanner shook himself out of his swoon forcefully, moving them on their way again.

"Mm, that was yummy," Josh hummed, snuggling against Tanner's body as they strolled.

"Okay, that's enough." Tanner released his hold on Josh and stepped away from him. He set the surfboard down against the tower, and walked up the ramp. Tanner entered the shady hut and removed a bottle of water from his backpack, guzzling it. He found the log sheet and balanced the bottle on the counter's edge. Before he began his entry, he relived the touch of their lips and the sensation of Josh's hands on his ass. "This is so not good."

※※

His hip hurting him, Josh kept slipping his hand into his suit to rub at the ache.

"You're sore aren't you?"

"Yeah. Just my hip."

"Let me see."

Josh peeled down his suit.

"You're already bruising. Better put some ice on it. It's getting purple." Tanner crouched lower to inspect it.

Josh pulled his bathing suit farther down, exposing his pubic hair and the top of his ass.

Tanner met his eyes quickly.

Josh winked, mouthing silently, "More?" He flashed his ass at him.

Not missing a beat, Tanner slapped it. "Behave." Tanner wagged his finger at Josh.

The swat gave him an instant erection. He craved another. Knowing Tanner's back was blocking the view to his naked ass, Josh whispered, "See me tonight."

"You should ice it. You want a cold pack to hold on it?" Tanner rubbed at the bruise gently.

"Later." Josh dragged his suit even lower, exposing the base of his hard cock.

Tanner gripped the waistband and pulled it up.

"Party pooper." Josh grinned wickedly.

"You are too insatiable."

"You have no idea." Josh rubbed his crotch, tempting Tanner's eyes to follow the gesture. Josh had a feeling he may finally be getting to him. Tanner seemed more interested than ever before.

As the sun started to set, Josh watched as Destiny, Joe, and Nathan found their way to his tower. He checked the time. The day was done. They walked back as a group to section headquarters, catching each other up on their day.

Tanner handed in his paperwork at headquarters. He knew Josh would be waiting. It was becoming a part of their routine. Tanner waved goodbye to the sparse evening crew, looped his backpack over his shoulder and left the building. Josh was standing on the top cement step, gazing out at the horizon, looking like an ad for men's cologne or a spread in Playgirl.

"Mr. Elliot," Tanner said as he approached.

"Come to my place."

The request was almost dire in its intensity. Tanner was petrified to be alone with Josh. About to decline, Tanner bit his lip, then he met Josh's pleading eyes.

"Tanner..." Josh's hand hovered over Tanner's chest as if it took all his will power to avoid touching it.

The battle broke out in Tanner's brain. He shifted his weight side to side as the indecision raged in him. Tanner was afraid of what would happen if they were on their own again. The yearning he felt these last few days was so draining. The need to connect with Josh was becoming a full time obsession.

Tanner couldn't imagine kissing a man, let alone allowing one to make him come. But the press of Josh's lips against his drove him crazy.

"Come here." Josh directed Tanner to his car. With his key fob, Josh unlocked the doors, opened the passenger's side for Tanner, and waited for him to get in before he walked around to the driver's side.

Sitting in the seat of Josh's car, Tanner was already nervous. He rested the backpack at his feet and waited as Josh climbed in, started the ignition, lowered the radio's volume and turned on the air conditioning.

Josh kicked off his flip-flops and twisted in his seat to face Tanner.

Tanner jumped out of his skin when Josh reached for his hand.

"Wow. I've never seen you this jumpy." Josh interlaced his fingers with Tanner's.

Unable to control his breathing, Tanner looked at his canvas backpack, anywhere but at Josh's gorgeous features and body.

"Tanner?"

"Yes, Josh?" Tanner felt his skin tingle from the cool air blowing on him and Josh's grip on his hand.

"Oh, Tanner Cameron?" Josh sang.

Tanner slowly raised his eyes to connect with Josh's green orbs.

Josh smiled. "I never thanked you."

"It's all right."

"No. I need to. Just between us. Man to man."

"Man...to..." Tanner moved his mouth to form the words but no sound emerged.

Josh released his grip on Tanner's hand and cupped Tanner's jaw in both of his. "Tanner."

Feeling the hairs rise on the back of his neck, Tanner was riveted to Josh's luminous eyes. "Yes, Josh."

"Thank you for helping me."

"You're welcome, Josh." He sounded like a robot. What the hell was the matter with him? Josh closed his eyes and leaned forward. Tanner knew what was coming and still did nothing.

Josh's lips connected to his. Tanner felt the zap of electricity down to his toes. Without tongues, they pressed their mouths together, almost like Tanner had done on the beach to feel Josh's breath.

Josh's fingers dug into Tanner's hair as Josh just touched his mouth against his.

Tanner was so excited he was about to combust. His cock was throbbing down the leg of his swimsuit, his skin was awash with chills, and his body was going into virtual meltdown. *I am kissing a man. I am kissing a—No. I am kissing the fantastic Josh Elliot who everyone wishes they were kissing.*

Josh sat back, as if checking his reaction.

Tanner felt like a dog panting in the heat.

Josh closed his eyes and went back for more.

*Goddamn it! Oh, fuck me, fuck me. I must want this.*

Tanner made a sound the minute Josh's tongue very gently touched his lips. The noise echoed in Tanner's head. He was whimpering for God's sake!

Tanner shook from nerves, or out of excitement, out of lust. He didn't know. Tanner allowed this luscious god to do as he wished, and he felt helpless in his hands.

Tanner's lips quivered under Josh's probing tongue. The urge to open his mouth became overwhelming. Unable to prevent the power of the attraction, Tanner tried not to believe anyone could see into this car, which was absurd. Anyone who stopped for a gape surely could.

The minute he unlocked his jaw, Josh's tongue entered his mouth. Tanner's fists clenched on his lap, and his eyes sealed shut. He allowed Josh's tongue to penetrate his body. It shook Tanner to the core. Another whimper escaped his chest and he wondered if he sounded like a lost little woman. He clutched his own crotch and squeezed as it throbbed and pressed against the fabric of his swimsuit.

Josh's hand cupped over his softly.

"*No,*" Tanner cried in agony.

His desperate plea made Josh back up to inspect his face.

Tanner gasped for breath. Sweat poured down his temples even with the air conditioning blowing out of the vents. "Oh God…oh God…"

Josh sat back, releasing all contact.

"I'm kissing you. Why am I kissing you?" Tanner swallowed down his terror.

"Tanner, I am so in love with you."

Tanner tightened his hold on his own dick. He knew he'd once again have to race home and jack off in a cold shower. All he had to do was get out of the car. "In...in love?"

"Hook, line, and sinker, Tanner. I'm way over my head."

"How can you love me?" Tanner felt like Josh's words were echoes from some canyon. He was completely out of his element here and didn't know whether to cry in shame or jump for joy at Josh's admission.

"How? Are you kidding me, Tanner?" Josh smiled lovingly. "You're incredible. Do you want me to list your attributes?"

"No. Please don't." Tanner was shaking. He touched his mouth and it felt numb.

Josh's eyes darted to Tanner's crotch. A wet stain had appeared in the red material. The humiliation was killing Tanner. He needed to get out of Josh's car.

"Let me follow you home."

"No." Tanner felt his heart fluttering in his chest.

"What are you afraid of?"

"You. Us." Tanner looked out of the windshield quickly.

"Us? You mean what we'll do once we're alone?"

Tanner whispered, "Yes."

"Tanner, let me satisfy you. Please." Josh reached out to touch the hand Tanner used to cover himself.

Tanner looked down at the contact. His cock jerked and he could feel the pre-cum oozing out. "How can I let you? You don't understand."

"I understand better than you think." Josh breathed deeply, petting Tanner's hand.

"I'm not gay," Tanner moaned like he was in agony, trying to convince himself that.

It made Josh laugh softly. "Number five? Six? How many times have you said that to me?"

"Josh." Tanner shook his head.

"Okay, Tanner." Josh sat back again so he was not touching him. "That's it then. My days of mentoring with you are up. It was nice knowing you."

"No..." Tanner had to confess they were working together from now on. He just couldn't get the words to come out. It sounded like he was as attached to Josh as Josh was to him. "You...you and I..."

"Yes? You and I?"

"I've..." Tanner cleared his throat. "I've requested..." This was murder. He had to tell him. Josh would see his assignment first thing in the morning anyway. "Josh, I've asked for us to be assigned together." Tanner's heart skipped a beat.

"You what?" Josh gasped.

"I..." Tanner glanced back at him to see if he was angry.

He knew he should get out of the car before he did something crazy. He just couldn't move. "I...asked...I asked the captain for...you..."

"You did? You asked the captain for permission for me to stay with you?" Josh's eyes were like two glowing marbles.

"I did. I didn't think you would be upset."

"Upset?" Josh replied. "I'm delirious! Tanner, I adore you."

"I..." Tanner stared at Josh as Josh gazed back at him. Tanner kept rubbing at his crotch, knowing damn well he'd never been this excited in his life. Without thinking, Tanner lunged at Josh and connected to his mouth.

Josh grunted as he banged against the driver's side window from the force of Tanner's tackle.

His hand in Josh's hair, Tanner sucked at his mouth, craving his tongue, finally dipping into Josh's mouth hungrily with his.

Josh wrapped his arms around Tanner's neck, French kissing him, twirling his tongue around Tanner's in an erotic dance.

Tanner's cock began pulsating so hard he thought he was coming. Tanner gasped in shock, parted from the kiss and reached into his swimsuit. "Jesus!"

Josh's eyes were half-open. "We can't do this here," Josh hissed. "Let me come to your place. Or come to mine."

Tanner removed his hand to see the amount of cum on it. He couldn't believe how sticky it was.

Josh grabbed his fingers. Tanner choked in shock as he began licking and sucking the cum off. "Ah! Holy fuck!"

"Tanner!" Josh roared with frustration.

"My place." Tanner surrendered.

"Fine! Go!" Josh shoved him.

Tanner stumbled from the car, leaving his backpack behind. Dizzy, feeling like he was on an alternate plane, Tanner sat behind the wheel of his jeep, starting it.

He couldn't remember driving home. All he remembered was opening his front door with Josh prodding him to get inside.

The second Josh entered the living room, he threw Tanner's backpack aside, and dove onto Tanner. Josh sucked on Tanner's mouth, digging his hands into Tanner's swimsuit.

"God! Wait, wait!" Tanner's head was spinning.

"Wait? Are you insane?" Josh had Tanner's dick out of his swimsuit.

Trying to clear his head, Tanner wished he had time to weigh this out in his mind. Pro? Getting Josh to suck his cock. Con? Having Josh suck his cock!

"Am I gay?" Tanner asked desperately like it was a life or death question.

"No!" Josh said. "You've told me fifty times you're not!"

"I'm not." Tanner looked down at his exposed dick. He'd never seen it drip like that before. Ever. "You sure?"

"Will you shut up?" Josh sank to his knees and took the head of Tanner's cock into his mouth.

Tanner shouted out in surprise and reached back for a wall.

Even with Josh holding him around his hips, Tanner had to brace himself on the plasterboard over a side table. He looked down in awe as Josh sucked him hard and deep. "Holy shit!"

Tanner tightened his grip as Josh pulled his suit down. His ass cheeks were spread apart and Josh massaged them as he enveloped Tanner's dick to his pubic hair.

Tanner couldn't believe it. No woman had ever been this passionate about giving him head, nor had the intense deep throating technique Josh did. Or… was quite as beautiful as this man was.

A delightful churning began in Tanner's balls. "I hope you're ready, Josh, because…" Tanner couldn't hold back. "Ah! Sweet mother of God!" His knees gave out and he shot his load into Josh's mouth.

Tanner had no idea how Josh had managed to swallow all of it. Not only had he gulped it down, Josh was sucking every last drop.

Tanner felt like he was about to pass out. He'd never had an orgasm that intense, and certainly had never been blown like that in his life.

Tanner collapsed at the knees, reaching for the floor. He felt it with his fingers and dropped back on the living room carpet, trying to breathe. *Christ! Augh! I'm doomed! I loved it. Oh, God help me he hasn't even sucked my damn balls yet.*

His hands resting on his chest, Tanner was literally gasping for air from nerves and excitement. It felt as if he were about to have a coronary. *Your mouth, oh, Josh Elliot, your fucking mouth. I'm so in trouble.*

Tanner groaned in agony and rubbed his eyes like they ached, but they didn't ache, he was still recuperating from the intensity that was beyond his comprehension.

⁂

Josh was in heaven leaning over Tanner's prone form. He softened his sucking to a gentle mouthing, and made sure he cleaned out the slit with his tongue, savoring the taste of Tanner's cum.

Josh let Tanner's cock slip out of his mouth. He lapped at it like a kitten with a bowl of milk, inhaling his crotch, moaning at the scent of him. Josh burrowed into Tanner's balls in delirium. "Tanner, you are delicious."

Josh removed Tanner's bathing suit completely and smiled at Tanner's weary gaze. Josh wriggled between his legs for more, like a starving man who had finally been served his feast. He lapped at Tanner's sack, licking the salty taste of the ocean off his skin. As he drew near his pink, puckered rim, he felt Tanner tense up. Josh slowed his voracious appetite to go down on him as he would like, and instead of plunging his entire tongue inside Tanner's ass like he wanted to, he teasingly tantalized it with the tip.

Josh lazily tickled his fingers along Tanner's taut skin, massaging his balls lovingly, cupping his limp cock in his palm.

Another low groan echoed in the room. Tanner whimpered in agony as Josh showed him the benefits of loving someone of the same sex. Josh sucked on one of Tanner's testicles, rolling it over his tongue, delicately tugging at the soft tissue. The pliable dick under Josh's hand pulsated and began to grow.

Josh ground his own cock into the carpet below, writhing in ecstasy at finally gnawing on the man he was madly in love with.

※

Tanner could do nothing but lie back and receive. Slightly shell-shocked, completely flabbergasted at Josh's ability, Tanner blinked in wonder at this secret Josh revealed—how a man sucks cock. Holy shit.

That naughty tongue kept being drawn to his ass. It tickled the rim causing Tanner's dick to reharden. His breathing beginning to deepen, Tanner kept still, stunned at the tongue lashing he was getting. He could get addicted to this and that scared the hell out of him. A hot wet mouth consumed his balls, one at a time. It was glorious, better than Tanner had imagined. He swooned like a teenager with his first kiss. A long low moan escaped his lips and he spread his legs wider. Tanner felt like shouting, *Eat me!* but was terrified to admit how much he was enjoying this contact. *I'm insane. I'm insane. I'm letting a guy suck my dick! You think this doesn't make you gay, Tanner? Think again!*

Josh's entire tongue entered his ass. Tanner gasped and shivered. His eyes were wide as they stared at the ceiling but were looking at nothing while his mind was on overload. Josh stroked Tanner's cock lovingly as that incredible tongue penetrated him.

"Ah!" Tanner's hips elevated off the floor involuntarily. Not knowing what to do with his hands, Tanner clenched his fists, flapped his arms like wings, finally lacing his fingers behind his head to prop it up so he could see this gorgeous creature devouring his genitals like no one ever had before.

Tanner felt something other than a tongue enter his anus. "Josh?" Through the wetness it massaged his ring, relaxing it. "Joshua? What are you…" *doing to me, you sex god? Augh! Oh my fucking god!* Goose bumps covered Tanner's skin and his dick went crazy, swelling and oozing.

A bursting sensation of pleasure shot through Tanner's body. It caught him completely by surprise and his hips thrust into the air as his dick grew completely solid. "What the hell are you doing? What are you touching? What the hell!" The impulse to come was suddenly so strong, Tanner closed his eyes and arched his back. "Mother-fucker! Josh!"

It amazed Tanner that this experience could make him crave more and fill him with terror at the same time.

"Oh, God!" Tanner jerked his hips up as his ass was penetrated deeper. And the deeper it went, the more pleasure Tanner experienced. "What the fuck? What the fuck?" he gasped, his head spinning as Josh found secret spots to make him lose his grasp on reality.

※

Josh knew he was being very naughty. But he just had to share this with Tanner. Had to. What if this was the only time he would get to do this? For all he knew Tanner would be so shell-shocked by the event he'd move out of state. There was no way Josh was going to miss a thing. He had Tanner where he wanted, and Tanner wanting more. It was a dream.

Josh felt Tanner unclench, and he pressed his slick finger against the magic spot over and over. The moment Tanner jerked his hips up and gasped, Josh came in his pants he was so hot.

Using his tongue in tandem with his finger, Josh kept Tanner's hole slick and wet. He reached around for Tanner's cock, and bumped into Tanner jacking off frantically.

Going for it, Josh burrowed into Tanner's ass cheeks, keeping him dripping wet as he ran one finger inside to the root of his pleasure, all the while massaging his balls in his palm.

Under his lips he felt Tanner's testicles tighten and his cock going into a spasm of another climax. Josh thrust his finger in and out to prolong the pleasure, stopping the minute Tanner ceased fisting himself furiously.

Josh rested his cheek on Tanner's thigh and caught his breath, relaxing his jaw and tongue muscles.

Tanner milked his cock slowly from his second orgasm. He was so stunned by the turn of events he couldn't move let alone say something. What was he to say? *Oh, my God, how did you make me come like that?*

Josh crawled up Tanner's body and lapped the spent cum off Tanner's chest and abdomen. Tanner allowed his head to rest on the floor. Tanner closed his eyes and tried to return to earth. *Oh, my God. I feel like a fucking virgin. No one has ever done anything like this to me in my life.*

Tanner couldn't stop the feeling of disorientation and knew it was adrenalin. Fear, mortal terror. How could he love this act? How could he come that hard? Twice?

Moaning and knowing this was going to change his life permanently, Tanner went limp against the floor and tried to get his heart rate back to a more normal rhythm.

Finally Josh made it all the way up his torso, collapsing on top of him until they were nose to nose. Tanner wrapped his arms around him, feeling like he could sleep where he was. He was completely sexually satisfied, and exhausted.

Josh nuzzled into his neck crooning, "I love you, I love you."

Tanner smiled. It felt so good to hear those three words. How long had it been since someone said that to him?

# Chapter Nine

They lay entwined on the carpet for a long while. Josh listened to Tanner's pounding heart as it drummed against his own. Feeling Tanner move under him, Josh raised his head from Tanner's chest and met his eyes.

"Josh."

"Tanner?" Josh smiled, they seemed to play the name game a lot.

"Holy shit. Josh…" Tanner shook his head.

Though he loved the feel of pressing his crotch against Tanner's, Josh rolled to his side to allow Tanner to get up if he chose. Lying calmly, Josh caressed Tanner's chest in adoration. "Was it nice?" Josh knew damn well it was fantastic.

"Wow." Tanner licked his lips, which looked dry from all the exertion.

As Tanner made a move to sit up, Josh backed away, allowing him.

Tanner leaned his weight on one hand and looked down at his naked body.

Seeing him growing modest, Josh reached for Tanner's bathing suit which was at his feet on the carpet, and handed it to him.

"Thanks, but I feel like I should shower and change." Tanner covered his crotch with the suit.

"I know the feeling. I came in my pants."

"Did you?" Tanner's eyes lit up in amusement.

"Yup." Josh smiled shyly.

They motivated themselves to stand. It was slow and unsteady for both of them. Tanner reached for the side table for balance. "You want to shower first?"

Josh wanted them to shower together, but had a feeling that may be pushing his luck. Tanner most likely would be shaken and apprehensive now.

"No. You go." Josh tilted his head.

"You sure?"

"Yeah. I'll just amuse myself for a few minutes."

"Go get something to drink. Just help yourself."

"Thanks."

"Oh, and there's a bathroom right around there if you need it."

Josh nodded. The awkwardness was back.

He watched Tanner walk down the hall, still covering his crotch. Tanner's ass was absolutely perfect, even with the redness from the minor rug burn.

Once he vanished, Josh shook himself out of his dream and headed to the bathroom. He slipped off his bathing suit and stuck it under the tap to rinse off the semen that had filled it, wringing it, shaking it out. He set it aside to wipe his skin off with some toilet tissue before putting it back on. Then he found his eyes in the mirror. "This is a one off deal, isn't it?"

Another emotion was creeping in. Guilt. Had he done something to Tanner that Tanner really didn't want?

That thought agonized him. The last thing he wanted to do was make Tanner uncomfortable around him.

"What did I do?" Josh had a feeling he had just fucked up their friendship, and it made him sick to his stomach.

Tanner waited for the shower to heat up, feeling a little nauseated. The regret formed in him instantly. "What the hell just happened?" Stepping into the shower, he allowed the water to pelt his face and leaned his hands against the tile trying to think.

*I just let Josh Elliot give me head. I have got to be out of my mind.*

He ran over the events preceding it to decide how it could have occurred. There were so many opportunities for him to abort the plan. Tanner grew upset with himself for being swept up by Josh's charm. *I don't want to be fucking gay. I can't be.*

Tanner imagined the people he worked with finding out, or his parents, his ex-wife, his good friends... It was a nightmare.

Tanner knew Josh was waiting for him. He had no idea where this little affair was leading. Hearing Josh declare his love for him, though he felt swept up in the moment, it scared the hell out of him. Tanner didn't know if he was capable of giving Josh back what he needed. Which he imagined was a real relationship with all the responsibilities of one. Plus they were going to work together. The two of them. Alone in that tower for ten hours a day. He shut the water off and stepped out of the tub.

"I can't have a relationship with another guy. Can I?" Tanner rubbed a towel over his back and stared in the mirror. "Are you gay? Bi? What the hell are you now, Tanner?"

Josh stood in Tanner's kitchen, drinking a glass of orange juice. A photo hung on the fridge with magnets, Tanner with what appeared to be his family. An older couple, possibly his mom and dad, and two young women. Sisters? Josh didn't think Tanner would have a photo of his ex lingering.

As he waited for Tanner to return, Josh had a bad feeling Tanner would ask him to leave. Though the sex was amazing, Josh wondered if Tanner's fear of being labeled would scare him to death. Josh knew that feeling first hand. Coming out was never easy. His family was not what he would call supportive. They tolerated it and cringed when he discussed it.

Josh was trying to prepare himself for the inevitable let down. A macho man like Tanner would have a very rough time accepting this new change. Then he remembered something Tanner had said in the car. Tanner had requested they work together? How could that be? What would happen now? After what Josh had just done to Tanner. Would he reconsider?

Tanner entered the room. Josh turned to face him. He was dressed in a pair of dark blue gym shorts and an LA Fire Department t-shirt.

"I helped myself to some juice." Josh held up his glass.

"Good. You must be hungry. I'll get us something to eat while you shower."

"Uh, actually, I was able to wash my suit out in the bathroom sink."

Tanner glanced down at it. "Now you're wet. You want a pair of shorts?"

"No, it's okay."

"You sure?"

"All right." Josh felt like the biggest pain in the ass on the planet.

Tanner left the room. Josh heard him climbing the stairs. He felt like crap and wondered if he should offer to leave. End this fiasco.

A moment later, Tanner returned with a pair of running shorts.

Josh set his glass down and was about to just exchange them where he stood, but thought better about it and headed to the bathroom. This was agony. He had just blown the guy and he couldn't change in front of him. Josh had no idea how to handle it. This straight guy was confusing the heck out of him.

~~

Tanner removed a glass from the cabinet and filled it with juice. He swigged it down thirstily and wondered what the hell they were supposed to do now? Shack up? Date? What?

Finished with his juice, he began digging for some food for dinner. With the refrigerator door open, Tanner noticed a tan pair of legs appear behind it. He stood upright and met Josh's eyes. "They fit okay?"

"Yeah. Good enough."

"What are you hungry for? I don't have a lot in the house. Should I call for Chinese food?"

"Tanner."

"Josh?" Tanner shut the fridge door.

"Do you want me to leave?"

That gave Tanner the opportunity to get out of this mess instantly. Did he want to take it?

Staring at Josh's forlorn expression, seeing the hurt in his eyes, Tanner felt miserable. Why was he acting so cold? He genuinely adored Josh.

"No. Come here."

Josh fell against his chest and embraced him, squeezing him tight. Tanner sniffed Josh's hair and sighed deeply. "I'm sorry. I don't know how to react. It's a bit of an overload."

"I know. Believe me. I'm feeling very confused myself, Tanner."

Tanner laughed sadly. "I'm not sure how I'm supposed to feel."

Josh leaned back so Tanner could see his eyes. "It seems like I pushed you into something you didn't want to do."

Tanner replied, "No. You didn't push me. You did seduce me." Tanner smiled wryly. "But I'm no pushover, Josh."

"Do you regret it?"

"Yes and no."

"Shit. That's not good. Tell me why you don't regret it and skip the part why you do."

Tanner combed Josh's thick hair back from his eyes. "Typical Josh Elliot just wants to know the good news."

"Hell yeah." Josh laughed.

Tanner broke their embrace and leaned back against the counter by the sink. "Fine. I don't regret it because I really like you. And…I did enjoy it."

Josh touched Tanner's arm gently. "All right. What's the bad news?"

Tanner met his eyes. "I'm not sure I'm the type to pursue a gay relationship, Josh." Tanner knew it wouldn't be fun to hear, but he was unprepared for Josh's reaction. It appeared to be a major blow.

"Yes. Right. I understand."

"Josh… Don't leave." Tanner followed him to the living room.

Josh held up his hand to stop him. "Look. Let me cut my losses. The more I hang around with you, the more I love you."

"I don't want you to go." Tanner couldn't believe he was saying that. Josh was right. The more time they spent together the more Tanner wanted him.

"To be honest, Tanner…" Josh met his eyes with an effort. "I shouldn't work with you any longer."

"No. Don't say that." Tanner was now on the receiving end of the blows.

"Are you kidding me?" Josh shook his head. "How the hell am I going to stop wanting you? Especially now. I've tasted your cock. Your ass. Your cum. I'm fucking hooked."

With each statement regarding what Josh had indeed sampled, Tanner felt his cock once again begin to throb. He was echoing the same thoughts in his mind. *You had me like no other human being has had me. No one has done what you did to me. Where do I go from here?*

But all Tanner could come up with verbally was, "Josh, you're my best guard. I can't lose you."

Josh blinked in disbelief. "That's why? Because of my lifesaving skills? Are you fucking joking?" He threw up his hands and headed to the door.

"No! Josh." Tanner grabbed him and drew him back from the exit. "Please don't storm out like this."

Josh spun around and confronted him. "What the hell do you want from me, Tanner? Have your cake and eat it? Huh? Toy with the gay guy, use him at work to get the job done, and don't reciprocate his feelings? Give me a break. Maybe you can separate your emotions like that, but I sure as hell can't."

"You sound like a woman." Tanner smiled, trying to break the tension and make Josh laugh. But it backfired.

"Fuck you." Josh attempted to escape again.

"Get back here." Tanner grabbed him around the waist.

As Josh leaned away, Tanner dragged him to the sofa, roughly forcing him to drop down on it.

"What?" Josh moaned in frustration. "Don't fuck with my head, Tanner."

The thought of Josh leaving his life permanently, transferring away, disappearing, was harder to swallow than Tanner wanted to admit. Maybe he did like him a hell of a lot.

"Josh."

"Tanner. Your turn to say 'Josh' again."

Tanner grabbed his face and kissed him, stunning Josh.

Josh gasped, "Holy shit. Don't start something you can't finish."

"Calm down. I swear dealing with you is like lighting a fuse on a firecracker." Tanner released Josh's face and held his hands on his lap. "Now…" Tanner caught his breath. "You keep losing sight of the fact that I have never touched a guy sexually before."

"Are you nuts? You've told me a hundred times you're not gay? Get real, Tanner."

"Yes, I've told you, but you think suddenly now that I've had one…"

"One…" Josh waited as Tanner struggled. "One amazing fucking blowjob…"

Choking, Tanner nodded. "One of those…that I can flip some internal gay switch and dive into the lifestyle."

"Why can't you?"

"Josh. Listen to yourself. You've been with guys all your life. Think about having a sexual fling with a woman."

"Ew."

Tanner blinked. "Really? That bad?"

"Yes."

Shaking his head to get back to the point, Tanner replied, "Yes, exactly. Previously my thoughts on touching a man were, 'ew'."

"No!"

"Yes! Josh, I didn't even think about it."

"Not once? Not while you were a teen? Didn't you go to day camp?"

"Camp?" Tanner tried not to get sidetracked. "Stop… listen to me. No. Not ever."

"Wow. I thought most straight guys did something gay at least once in their lives."

"What? Where the hell did you hear that?" Tanner looked down as Josh tugged one of his hands free and started stroking Tanner's thigh.

"I don't know. Isn't it common knowledge?"

"No! Josh…slow down," Tanner said.

"I can't. I'm so turned on by you."

"Okay." Tanner trapped his roving hand. "Hear me out, please, Josh."

"Sorry. Go on. Touching men is icky for you. Goody. Tell me more."

Not reacting to Josh's expression of annoyance, Tanner gathered his thoughts. "I am trying to see the world through your eyes, Josh, but you need to do the same back. I've already mentioned I've never even had a close gay friend to ask questions about that lifestyle. I suppose I never thought much about it. Then..." Tanner sighed heavily. "You came along."

"Oh?" Josh's expression turned seductive.

"Stop. Listen with the head on your shoulders not the one in your pants."

"Your pants. I'm in your gym shorts."

"Whatever. Look…I'm not going to deny I…" Tanner could see Josh hanging on his every word. "I…like you."

"Mm?"

"Yes. A lot."

"Okay."

"And…and that kissing you…and…" Tanner felt his cheeks heat up horribly. "You know."

"No. I don't."

"Josh."

"Tanner. Your turn."

"Stop. You're not helping me."

Josh threw up his hands. "What am I supposed to be helping you do? If you think I'm going to agree with the little angel in your head and pretend that what we did was satanic and you should run miles away. Forget it."

"That would be helpful," Tanner teased, noticing Josh was not amused. "Sit still! Jesus, you're a live wire!" Tanner tried to trap him to the sofa. "Your parents must have had a really hard time with you as a kid."

"You have no idea."

"Don't I? Now sit still and let's deal with this!" Tanner released Josh slowly as if he would bolt if freed.

"Fine. Deal. But the question I want to ask is…"

Tanner held his hand.

"Are you going to want it again? Huh? Can I do it to you again?"

*Oh, fuck yeah.* That's what Tanner wanted to say. *Another blowjob like that? Are you kidding me?* But he was terrified. What next? Another? Another? Yet another? Josh's mouth constantly connected to his genitals? How often? Every night?

"Tanner?"

"Uh…"

"Oh, Tanner? Anyone home?"

"I'm thinking."

"It's not a trick question!"

"Yes, it fucking is!" Tanner gulped in anxiety.

"I get it." Josh grinned. "You fucking loved it and you hate the fact that you fucking loved it."

Nailed. Tanner stammered, but nothing tangible came out.

"So…" Josh leaned closer, over Tanner's lap. "You're afraid that because you 'fucking loved it' that we'll keep doing it. And you'll suddenly be 'gay'."

"In a nutshell. Yes." Tanner swallowed audibly as Josh smoothed his hands closer to his crotch.

"So…and correct me if I'm wrong…" Josh ran one finger over Tanner's growing bulge. "You'd rather convince yourself that you can live without another 'amazing fucking blowjob' just so the world will know that Tanner Cameron is pure, unadulterated heterosexual."

"Why, when you put it that way, do you make me sound so lame?" Tanner peeked down as Josh's finger drew circles on his thickening cock.

"Your choice, handsome." Josh moved in front of him. "Just remember. Once you have a taste of the forbidden fruit…well, I think you can finish that sentence."

Just imagining Josh's mouth on his, tongues dueling, and his fingers stroking his cock, Tanner couldn't control himself. "What is it about you?"

"You tell me," Josh crooned, using the tip of his tongue to tease Tanner's lips.

"I can't. I can't explain it. And I feel as if I need to." Tanner eased back from Josh's advance. "Why? Why you? What is it about you that has made me…"

"Want a man?"

Josh didn't relinquish his caressing of Tanner's taut bulge. "Yes!" Tanner peeked down at Josh's roving fingers again. He felt like screaming, 'I want you to keep sucking my balls and licking my ass,' but panted to control himself instead.

"Do you think I'm good looking?"

"Duh. What am I, an idiot?"

"Do I smell nice?"

Tanner inhaled him and moaned, "God yeah."

"Does my personality flip your on button?"

"Yes. But why?"

"I'm getting there. And you say I'm impatient?" Josh began kissing Tanner's jaw. "Do you like the way my body looks?"

Tanner felt his Adam's apple bob mid-swallow as Josh skimmed his teeth over it. "Yes." That one was painful to admit.

"When I touch you, do you shiver?"

Tanner closed his eyes. "Yes." This talk suddenly felt like truth or dare.

"Have you thought about me while you've jacked off?"

Turning his face aside as Josh continued to run kisses up and down his neck and jaw, Tanner was in heat. "Yes…" he breathed very softly.

"Do you want me to suck on your dick again?"

A chill washed up Tanner's spine and made him shiver. "Yes."

"Then you, my friend, just may be a sodomite." Josh sat back, smiling dreamily at him.

Tanner urged Josh to lie back on the sofa, trapping him underneath his weight, closing his eyes. Tanner opened his lips and met Josh's. At the touch, Tanner was covered with tingles. They kissed that way, long, slow, and deliberate, as if discovering the dark secrets of the long journey ahead.

It was useless fighting it. Tanner wished he could turn his back on Josh and pretend this was idle curiosity. But that would be a lie.

This wasn't some pick up in a bar. He and Josh had become friends first.

Tanner admired and liked him. A lot.

Tanner smiled at Josh. "And we still haven't had dinner."

A lazy smile formed on Josh's soft lips. From under Tanner, Josh straddled his knees around Tanner's waist. Tanner knew his throbbing dick was pressing against Josh's ass. He couldn't visualize what fucking Josh would be like. That image was as foreign to Tanner as Saturn's moons.

Josh slid his hands into the back of Tanner's shorts, massaging his bottom hungrily.

"I've already come twice," Tanner said. "Three? In an hour? That would tie my all time record for the most orgasms in a twenty-four hour period."

"Lightweight," Josh teased.

"Really?" Tanner shivered as Josh's hand stroked his ass crack.

"Really." Josh ran his tongue over Tanner's chin.

Josh's erection pushed up into him. Tanner was glad Josh had come on his own earlier, because he wasn't sure he was ready for that hurdle yet. But...Josh was obviously horny and Tanner was one orgasm up on him. How did this gay-thing go? A climax for a climax?

"Do...do you want to eat?"

"Yes." Josh squirmed under him.

"Was that seductive answer for Chinese food or?"

"Or." Josh lowered his eyelids and opened his lips.

Tanner thought Josh was so sexy he was about to explode. "What right do you have to be this damn gorgeous?" Tanner dug his hand into Josh's hair.

"What right do you have to make me insane?" Josh humped Tanner from underneath.

Anxiety washed over Tanner. "I...I don't know if I can...to you...yet." Tanner knew he sounded like a babbling fool.

"I'm not asking you to...yet."

"Then...then how am I?" Tanner made a move to sit back.

Josh stopped him. "Shut up. Let me grind. Kiss me again." Josh slipped his hand down his shorts to straighten his cock.

"You're going to come in my pants now?" Tanner chuckled softly.

"You want me to take them off? Come on you?"

"Uh..."

"Then shut up." Josh drew Tanner's face down, connecting to his mouth.

Envisioning Josh being able to come during their kissing caused Tanner to shiver in delight. He wanted to know when Josh was ready to climax so he could enjoy it with him. Tanner whispered, "Am I doing okay?"

"Yes." Josh's eyes were sealed shut as he worked his body under Tanner's.

"Tell me...when...when you..."

Josh's eyes blinked open. "Yes! You fantastic man!" Josh wrapped his arms around Tanner's neck and mashed his lips against Tanner's.

Tanner had no idea his words would have that effect. As Josh went wild under him, grinding and humping to his heart's content, Tanner wondered what it would feel like, skin to skin. His own dick was again primed. Would Josh suck it?

"Josh..." *Please suck me again...*

"Tanner," Josh answered, still connected to Tanner's lips.

"Let's take off our shorts."

Josh jolted, pulling back to stare. "Really? You sure?"

"Seems silly to mess up two pairs of clean shorts."

Josh scrambled to get off the couch, almost as if he expected Tanner to change his mind. With a quick flick of his wrist, Josh was naked, holding his own dick and working it gently.

"Holy shit." Tanner stared at him in awe. "Maybe I'm jumping the gun."

"No! No, Tanner. Don't get cold feet." Josh leaned forward and kissed him again. "You don't have to touch me with your hand." He urged Tanner up on the sofa, getting back to his place underneath, dragging Tanner down.

Tanner hadn't removed his shorts, but knowing Josh was naked under him made his head spin. Before he said another word to stop what was happening, Josh lips were against his.

Battling with his ego, his fear, his attraction, the label, the sense of right and wrong, Tanner was breaking down once more, until...

Until he felt Josh's body experience an orgasm.

Josh rammed quick hard thrusts against Tanner's cock.

Opening his eyes quickly, Tanner stared down at Josh as his brow furrowed, his teeth showed under his top lip, and his crotch convulsed in quick spasms under him.

"Ah! Ah! Oh, Tanner...oh..."

The sensation of Josh's pleasure rocked Tanner to the core. He never knew if his female partners came or, for that matter, if they were faking it. He never asked. If he wasn't pleasing them, they needed to let him know.

But...

Josh's cum spurted out of him like a shower, spattering his chest and tight six-pack abs. Tanner gazed down on it in awe. No faking that.

"Tanner...oh, man..."

"You came just rubbing on me?"

"Rubbing your beautiful dick. Tanner, you get me so hot, I can come just thinking about you." Josh's green eyes seemed to glow.

Sitting back on his heels, Tanner stared down at Josh's naked flesh and the creamy white spatters as Josh caught his breath.

It was the strangest experience. Tanner was looking down at another guy's naked erection and sperm. A cock that was still bobbing from orgasm and slow to grow soft. Did it turn him on?

As if to see, Tanner placed his hand over his own cock. It was throbbing as well, and certainly not soft, not by a long shot. Then this must be turning him on. Or he'd be soft.

Tanner gave Josh his rapt attention, feeling him move. Still covered in his own cum, Josh got to his knees on the carpet and nudged Tanner's hand away.

This was going to happen again? Tanner's chest began to rise and fall rapidly. One time was a mistake, twice was a whim. Three times? A habit. And Tanner could tell Josh's mouth would be damn habit forming.

About to tell him no, Tanner felt the first heat and penetration into Josh's mouth. He shut his own on his protests. *Oh yes...suck it. My God I am loving this so much I can't believe it.*

Tanner shifted his position on the couch so he was relaxed in a wide straddle and able to observe Josh this time.

It was the look on Josh's face that floored him. Josh seemed to relish what he was doing. Pleasure emoted from his features. With just the tips of his fingers, Josh gently held Tanner's cock from moving as he lapped at the head and seeping slit. The sight of Josh's tongue on his erection was unreal to Tanner. Surreal.

Josh sank Tanner's cock all the way into his mouth causing Tanner's hips to thrust forward and his head dropped back on the sofa cushions. "Joshua Elliot. What on earth have you done to me?"

A humming sound of contentment from Josh made Tanner's dick shiver. Tanner battled the urge to keep his eyes closed and just allow his other senses to kick in. Tanner forced his head back up in order to look. Josh had a hand on either thigh, pushing outward to widen Tanner's straddle.

Josh began toying with his balls gently. Tanner's head fell back again and he moaned in exquisite agony. "You're making me addicted to your mouth, Josh Elliot. Stop making me swoon."

Another wicked hum made the hair stand on Tanner's arms. "Jesus, when you suck my balls..." Tanner whimpered as they were enveloped in a hot mouth and a tongue swirled around each. "Holy shit." Tanner loved it. He couldn't deny it.

The pressure of Josh's finger returned to his anus. Tanner was done for. *Oh here we go! Son of a bitch!* "Josh! Holy fuck!"

Tanner jerked his hips up and grabbed Josh's hair, fucking his mouth much harder than he ever would have dreamed of doing to a woman. As Josh stroked him internally making him dizzy, he came yet again.

Tanner's eyes shut tight, his teeth grinding at the intensity. He didn't know if he had anything left to give up, but something came out, he was certain of it.

A moment later, Josh was lapping at his cock like a Popsicle. Tanner moaned, "I haven't been this sexually gratified in a decade. What a mouth you have on you, Mr. Elliot. A very talented mouth."

Josh crawled up Tanner's body until their cocks were pressed together. Tanner felt his kisses on his neck and jaw. He draped his arms around Josh's back.

Josh's cock throbbed against his. It was the oddest thing he had ever experienced in his life. Another guy's cock touching his. Life was full of surprises.

"I'm so spent I can't even motivate myself to call for food."

"I'll do it." Josh kissed near his ear, whispering, "I love you so much, Tanner. Thank you."

"For what?" Tanner laughed weakly.

"For experimenting. I know how hard this was for you."

"If I had any energy, I'd agree with you."

Josh pecked his lips, hopped up, and returned with the telephone book and the cordless phone. "Who do you usually use?"

"How did you stand so quickly?" Tanner rubbed his face, looking at his sticky body. "Uh…I don't know. You think I have any brain cells left intact after today?"

"What about Little Asia?"

"Yes. That's the one." Tanner flipped his shorts up over his cock as it softened.

"Mongolian beef? Garlic shrimp? What do you want?"

"Yes. Fine. I can't think. You decide." Tanner stared at Josh, who was completely naked, holding the phone to his ear, looking like a sex god.

"I'll take care of it, cutie." He winked at Tanner and rubbed Tanner's thigh. "You just recover."

Tanner rested his head against the cushions again as Josh took care of business. Tanner stared at his sleek form as he strode without modesty back and forth in front of him, ordering food. "Yes, I'd like egg rolls, garlic shrimp with fried rice…"

Tanner smiled. It was nice having another man around to take over when he felt too tired. Anna never did. She refused to pull her weight, never sucked him off like that, never made him feel completely sated, loved, taken care of.

*Oh my God, I'm gay.*

# Chapter Ten

Thursday morning, Josh raced around getting ready for work. What a difference a day made. Since yesterday evening, giving head to Tanner *twice*! Making him come *three times*! Snuggling, giggling, sharing Chinese food, even feeding each other shrimp! He was in heaven. It was hard to leave Tanner and come home, but he had to. Sleeping over would come eventually. And even though Josh was anxious to move this relationship on to another level, he knew Tanner was struggling to keep up.

One week. It had taken one week and Josh had sucked Tanner's cock. How amazing was that? He was floating on a cloud.

Spinning, singing silly love songs, dancing and pumping his hips and fist into the air, Josh felt that wonderful sensation of infatuation and new love. It was exhilarating.

Josh skipped down the stairs to the parking garage, hopped into his convertible, Josh blasted Alanis Morissette's *Head Over Feet*, and sang it at the top of his lungs.

The white jeep was already parked in the lot. Josh grinned happily and closed his roof, snapping it into place. He snatched his backpack off the seat and flew down the cement steps.

Tanner was speaking with a supervisor. Josh smiled in delight, feeling his skin sizzle with passion as he ogled his tall, perfect physique. Just to be sure, Josh checked his assignment. He was scheduled to share the tower with Tanner, sure enough.

"Hey, Josh."

"Hi, Nathan."

"How are you feeling after yesterday?"

"Huh? Yesterday?" Josh tilted his head.

"Yes. Your hip."

"Oh. That's fine. Perfect."

"Hi, Josh, Nat." Two new seasonal recruits, Noah and Christopher stepped inside the room.

Josh barely knew the men even though they had trained together. The part-timers were mostly used to cover weekends, permanent staff sick days, and holidays.

"Hey." Josh smiled at them as they checked on their assignments.

"Supposed to be in the nineties today," Chris whispered. "Brutal."

"Bet some people get heatstroke." Noah crossed his arms.

"Just wait. We haven't even hit the peak of summer yet." Nathan shook his head. "I'm dreading the Fourth of July weekend."

Seeing Tanner approaching, Josh felt his skin cover with chills. Josh eyed Tanner's crotch, licking his lips, remembering the taste of his cum.

"Good morning." Tanner smiled. "Ready for a hot one?"

"Hell yeah." Josh made a face of ecstasy at him.

"Behave, Mr. Elliot." Tanner shook his finger at him.

Josh almost swiped it out of the air and sucked it. It took everything he had not to. It seemed Tanner realized it as well, taking it back quickly. "Right. Are we all walking out together?"

The group nodded in reply.

"Let's go." Tanner gestured to the door.

Josh hung back to walk with Tanner as they headed to the beach. "You still okay?" Josh whispered, dreading any bad feelings.

"Not at work."

Cut off abruptly, Josh wondered, *Why the hell not?* It would sure make the days more fun. "You really are a party pooper."

"Behave."

"You know that's unlikely." Josh winked.

Nathan fell in at his opposite side as they strolled to their respective towers. Nathan looked over at Tanner, then he gave Josh a smug smile, as if he suspected something because of the new assignment. It was rather bold of Tanner to request it. Josh wondered if anyone knew he had, or perhaps they thought it was just coincidence. He had no idea. If there was any fallout, Tanner had only himself to blame.

Josh kept his expression blank, though he was thinking, *Yes, I love this Adonis lifeguard. So?*

The minute Tanner's body brushed against his as they walked on the lumpy sand, Josh put his arm around his waist. No hesitation.

Tanner shot him a warning look and nudged his arm away.

It was evident Nathan had spied it because his head jerked toward the movement quickly.

"You are going to get us into trouble," Tanner whispered.

"What's going on?" Chris asked Nathan as he and Noah walked close by.

"Nothing," Nathan replied with tongue firmly pressed in his cheek.

Josh felt something tickling his hair. He spun around and found Nathan's playful grin. Silently Nathan pointed to Tanner and mouthed, "You and him?"

Josh said nothing, catching Tanner's suspicious eye.

Once they were closing in on their tower and Tanner was a few paces ahead of them, the three other men were about to part ways and head farther down the beach.

Before they did, Nathan nudged Josh. "You sly dog."

"What?"

"You and Tanner?"

Josh found Chris and Noah had paused on their way to listen curiously.

"Shut up, Nat." Josh cringed.

"Man. I never would have thought a guy as macho as Tanner could be gay."

Just as he said it, Tanner spun around before he entered the hut.

Josh felt his stomach sink. The expression on Tanner's face showed Josh he had overheard. He stared at Tanner for a moment, feeling his anger. *Shit.*

Before Nathan walked away, Josh grabbed his arm to whisper, "Why did you have to say that?"

"Huh?"

"Nat, you said that in front of Noah and Chris."

"Are you guys hiding it?"

"Hiding what, you dill hole! There's nothing going on. So shut up about it."

"Sorry. I thought you and him…you know. You're assigned together now. I thought it was a no brainer."

"You are a dipshit, you know that? I have no idea why we were assigned to the same tower. Probably just the luck of the draw." Josh felt ill. He wished someone would throw him a lifeline.

Josh watched the first glance of suspicion fall upon Tanner.

Noah and Chris were staring at Tanner as if he had suddenly grown horns.

"Your tower is that way," Tanner snarled, pointing down the coast.

Tanner entered the hut.

Josh knew Tanner wouldn't want the information made public. How had he managed to do it to him already? He had lectured himself on keeping their affair private. He knew damn well Tanner couldn't handle anyone thinking he was gay.

"Nat." Josh stopped him from walking away.

"What Josh?"

"It was just wishful thinking."

"Thinking about what?"

"About Tanner. There's nothing going on between me and Tanner. I wish!"

"Oh. I just thought with the two of you together…"

"He's straight, Nat. Like totally."

"I always thought so. But I mean someone as pretty as you could turn him gay. I bet if you seduced him, he'd say yes."

Josh replied, "He wouldn't say yes. He used to be married, Nat."

"Used to be. But he's single now." Nathan laughed wickedly. "How interesting. You two? Alone in a hut all day? Hm?"

Knowing Noah and Chris were still lingering, waiting for Nathan, Josh grabbed Nathan's shoulders and shook him. "Don't spread gossip, Nat. How would you like it if people said shit about you?"

"About me? I don't like guys, Josh. Everyone knows I'm hot for Samantha. It's so obvious."

"Then don't spread rumors about anyone else, okay?"

"You mean like you and Tanner are doin' it?" He laughed.

Josh peeked over his shoulder at Noah and Chris; they didn't seem to be paying attention as they talked together. He grabbed Nathan by the face and planted a kiss on him.

Nathan choked and flailed his arms around in panic.

Pulling back from the disgusting contact, Josh wiped his mouth and said, "There! You kissed a gay guy. You spread shit about Tanner. I'll spread shit about you."

"Sick!" Nathan spat on the sand. "You're fucking insane!"

"Shut up and just go to your tower." Josh winced, wiping his mouth on his arm.

"Why the hell did you do that?"

"To shut you the fuck up."

"You suck!"

"I know. But it'll teach you some fucking manners, asshole."

Tanner stepped out of the hut. "What did I miss?"

Noah and Chris were doubled over with laughter. "Josh kissed Nat!" Noah roared, wiping his eyes.

"What?" Tanner said. "You're joking."

"It was fucking hilarious," Chris laughed.

"What are you still doing here? Go to your own tower."

They shut up and finally left.

Tanner grabbed the binoculars that he had set on the rail, ignoring Josh.

Josh was glad that the other three men moved off. He wished he had mouthwash because the kiss made him want to spew. Josh prayed what he did would shut Nathan up and cause him to ruminate about the ills of gossip and innuendo.

After the odd incident, which Josh knew Tanner did not see, he looked back at Tanner who was using his binoculars to scan the water. Josh walked up the ramp to stand next to him. "Hey." He paused, waiting for Tanner's response. The glare he received shook him up. "Tanner?"

"Go get a can and walk the beach."

"What's eating you?" Josh asked, placing his hands on his hips. He noticed Tanner look in the direction the other three had gone. "Tanner, did you see—"

"Was it a nice kiss?" Tanner sneered.

"No, Tanner..." Josh laughed, about to explain.

"Fuck you. Get away from me."

"Wait. I was just—" Josh's words fell to silence as Tanner took off jogging. "No you fucking don't!" Josh sprinted after him. "Tanner!" Josh pumped his legs hard to catch up. "Tanner Cameron! You idiot! Stop and let me tell you what happened!"

Tanner increased his speed.

Josh knew he was no match for him in a race. Stopping, leaning over his knees to catch his breath, Josh watched as he vanished into the distance.

"Well, the good news is…you're jealous." Josh spun on his heels and walked back to the tower. He grabbed a rescue can and took a walk.

※

Josh didn't know how Tanner could avoid him for ten hours, but he had. Every time Josh found an opportunity to explain, Tanner left or jogged off. It was maddening.

At the end of shift, Josh stood by Tanner's jeep, blocking the driver's door. Finally Tanner showed up, still fuming.

"Move," Tanner ordered.

"Will you fucking listen to me?"

"I said move!"

Josh grabbed Tanner's shoulders. "I did it to shut him up."

"Fuck you. Don't touch me."

"He was beginning to find demented delight in the idea that you being my gay lover would be a fun rumor to spread." Josh didn't relinquish his hold. Tanner refused to look him in the eye. "So I swallowed my fucking disgust and kissed that ugly jerk-off. I wanted to stop him from gossiping about the man I love." Josh shook Tanner roughly. "He's revolting! He tasted like shit."

Tanner's angry glare found his.

"It was a desperate measure for a desperate situation." Josh softened his tone slightly. "If anything happened to you, I'd die. You get it? I would do anything, sacrifice my goddamn measly life to keep you out of hot water. And that includes trying to stem the flow of conjecture about you and me being a couple." Josh took a breath and tried to keep Tanner's attention. "Though I would gladly shout it from the rooftops, and wear a t-shirt saying Tanner's Fuck-buddy, I know you feel slightly different."

"Slightly."

Josh noticed a tiny curl at one corner of Tanner's mouth. "Slightly. Now pity me for having to kiss that schmuck for your benefit."

Tanner's posture relaxed and he stepped back. "Honest?"

Josh choked in amazement. "Do you think Nathan is attractive?"

"No."

"Thank you. Enough said. If I have to keep thinking about that nasty kiss, I'll vomit. Now. Your place or mine?"

"Yours."

"Better." Josh smiled. "Follow me." He walked to his car, grinning wickedly at Tanner as he did the same. Once he had backed out of the parking space and was on his way, Josh smiled excitedly. "You're jealous. How incredible is that?"

※

Tanner didn't realize how much the thought of Josh going with someone else upset him. But it did. He didn't want anyone else getting the benefit of Josh's body. Or his mouth.

The things Tanner needed in any sort of relationship, including with male friends, was trust and dependability.

Maybe Tanner was old fashioned that way. His parents had set the example for him. They had been together for nearly thirty-five years. Both his sisters were still married to their first husbands. Only Tanner had failed in his first marriage out of the three of them. Was it his fault that Anna changed her mind and wanted children and he didn't? That wasn't the only reason. He was sure she had been having an affair.

How convenient was it that the minute they were divorced she moved a man into their house? A man he had never met before. No one meets a man and moves in with him a month later, do they?

Tanner noticed Josh's car pausing at the gates of an underground parking garage. He passed beyond it and found street parking. He walked back to the same spot to see Josh waiting for him on the sidewalk, a big happy smile on his face.

*Am I in love with a gay man? Am I?*

Tanner didn't know anymore.

As he approached Josh, he heard him singing. Leaning closer to catch the lyrics he asked, "You're falling head over feet?"

"Do you know that one?" Josh asked, walking to the front of the apartment building. "That song by Alanis?"

"No. Sorry."

"Too bad." Josh unlocked the lobby door. "My place is on the third floor. Elevator or stairs?"

"Stairs."

"Martyr."

"You asked." Tanner followed Josh to the stairwell, staring at his ass as he took the steps two by two. He reached out to touch him. Josh paused and looked back. "Are you admiring my bottom?"

"Maybe." Tanner nudged him to keep moving.

"Want it?"

Tanner sighed uneasily. "Uh..."

Josh stood at his unit with the key. "It's not much of a living space. Don't get your hopes up."

"I'm not judging you, Josh." Tanner glanced around as Josh pushed the door back. It was tidy, well furnished, but small. He set his backpack down and walked to the window to have a look at the view.

"You can sort of see the San Gabriel's if you squint and tilt your head sideways."

Tanner laughed softly. "Sort of."

"Not a very nice view is it?"

"You'd have to pay for a view."

"True."

Josh surrounded Tanner from behind, hugging him. Tanner trapped Josh's arms, hugging him back.

"I'd never cheat on you."

"I'm sorry. Just when the guys saw you kiss Nat..."

"They saw me? Augh! That's just grand." Josh groaned in agony. "That reminds me. Hang on. Let me go brush my teeth and gargle. Brr."

As he released Josh, Tanner smiled at his antics, very glad kissing Nathan revolted Josh. The idea certainly disgusted him. Tanner shivered. "Yech. Nasty."

He relaxed on the sofa and picked up a book that sat on the low glass coffee table. His eyes widened in surprise. "*The Boys of Bel Ami?*" He flipped the pages and inhaled sharply at the sight of snuggling, naked, pretty boys with erect cocks photographed in black and white. "Zoiks!" He closed it and set it hurriedly back on the table. "This place is filled with landmines."

"Are you talking to yourself?"

"Yes!" Tanner remembered the comments about gay porn. "Christ." He rubbed his forehead. "What on earth have I gotten myself into?"

"I'm back. Here. Taste." He plopped down on the sofa and reached for a kiss. Tanner pecked his lips quickly.

"That wasn't much fun. Still grossing you out a little?"

"No. Uh, what's that?"

"It's a book, silly."

"A book of?"

"Naked men. So?"

"Whoa."

"You know, it only makes you more adorable when you blush." Josh hugged one of Tanner's arms to his chest. "Did you peek?"

"I did. Shocking. I never knew there were books like that around."

"Want to look at it with me?"

"Hell, no."

"Still gun shy?"

"What do you think?" Tanner rubbed his coarse jaw with his palm.

"Should I buy one with naked women?"

"No. Don't be absurd."

"Do you look at magazines like that?" Josh rubbed Tanner's thigh.

"Sometimes. I'm not addicted to images of naked women, don't worry."

"Thank God for that." Josh slipped his hand into the leg of Tanner's red swimsuit.

"Am I bi?"

"Why the hell do you need a label?" Josh snuck his fingers into Tanner's crotch.

"I don't know. I suppose I feel like I need some kind of stability."

"And being called straight, bi, or gay will give it to you?"

"Probably not. It'll probably terrify me."

"What the hell is so frightening about finding pleasure in another person? What am I missing here?"

"You've been brought up differently than me." Tanner looked at his lap, seeing Josh prospecting for gold in his swimsuit.

"How so?"

"I don't know. I assume you had a very liberal upbringing."

Josh made a buzzing sound. "Wrong. Next assumption?"

As Josh connected with his balls, Tanner widened his straddle. "So, you were brought up by conservatives?"

"Ding! Correct answer."

"Huh." Tanner's cock went rigid with Josh's probing digits. "Then how did you end up gay?"

"Like I fucking know?" Josh gave up on the tiny touches and reached boldly down the front of Tanner's suit.

Tanner's cock was squeezed, and he moaned softly. "How did you know you were gay?"

"He asks me this while I'm yanking on his beautiful erection. Oh, the irony."

"Jesus, Josh…you know just how to touch me." Tanner wanted to strip off his swimsuit and feel Josh's mouth again.

"We've got the same anatomy. You do say the most inane things. You sure you're a paramedic?"

"I'm not sure of a fucking thing at the moment." Tanner raised his hips off the sofa and peeked down at his cock as Josh played.

"I want you on my bed, please."

Tanner whipped his head toward him. "To do what?"

"Stop panicking. To suck you."

"Oh." Tanner wondered if he'd ever feel comfortable to do anything to Josh. It didn't seem very fair.

Josh stood, reaching out his hand. "Come, my beautiful prince."

Flipping his cock back into his swimsuit, even though it didn't fit inside any longer, Tanner stood, reaching for Josh's hand. He was escorted around a corner. It was a modest bedroom with a queen-sized bed, a dresser, a closet, and a television stand across from the foot of the bed. Tanner sat down on it, looking at the collection of DVDs. Leaning closer, he read the titles, "*Men with Big Toys? Big Drill?* Oh, dear."

"Come away. You'll go blind." Josh dragged Tanner up to his pillows. Tanner kicked off his canvas shoes and sat up against the headboard. "You've had a lot of guys, huh?"

"On the contrary. Three. Four if you count you, but I've yet to say I've 'had' you."

"Three?" Tanner watched as Josh removed his t-shirt and bathing suit. He was trying to get used to seeing him naked. It still felt slightly unsettling.

"Yes. Three. One in high school, one in college, one at my last job. One. Two. Three." He held up a finger for each.

"Really?"

Josh crossed his arms over his chest. "Did someone back home in Oreee-gone tell you all gay boys are whores?"

"I just thought…"

"You thought wrong." Josh sat on the bed and ran his finger over Tanner's chest to his nipple. "I have a high sex drive, Tanner, but I'm extremely picky."

"Really?"

"Uh huh." Josh drew a line down the center of Tanner's body to his belly button. "Will you take those off? Or too shy?"

Looking down at Josh's blushing cock, Tanner dragged the bathing suit off his legs and kicked it over the side of the bed.

"Look at you," Josh crooned. "You put my Bel Ami boys to shame."

"Your who?"

"The book of nudes. Never mind. Man, you get all forgetful when our clothing comes off."

"I can't get used to being naked with another man."

"You will. I hope. Does it still shake you up?"

"A little, but not as bad as it did yesterday. I guess I'm struggling with your expectations."

"I have none."

"None?" Tanner felt better already.

"No. I expect you'll do what you feel comfortable with and no more."

"Thank you, Josh."

"Don't mention it. Just being able to suck your cock is enough for me."

"How could it be?" Tanner touched Josh's cheek softly. "I feel bad that I can't do anything for you."

"Yeah?" Josh's wicked smile emerged.

"Now, hang on." Tanner laughed, holding up his hand.

"Want to jerk me off?"

"Uh. Does that mean I have to touch your dick?"

Josh chuckled. "Well, hm, how else could you do it? Mental telepathy?"

"I...I..." Tanner shrank back.

"How about this?" Josh held his own cock, bringing Tanner's hand to hold his hand. "Squeamish?"

"No. That's okay." Tanner adjusted his hold on Josh's knuckles.

"That's all well and good, but I'd like to devour yours first. You mind?"

"Hell, no."

"Good. Move over."

Tanner shifted on the bed as Josh crept down to lie between his thighs.

"I just love this." Josh inhaled him, rubbing his face against Tanner's balls.

"Me, too." Tanner shivered. Josh pressed his lips to Tanner's cock, running them up and down the length. "Wow. You are so good at this, Josh."

"Got straight A's in high school."

"Huh?"

"Nothing. Lie back and enjoy."

"No problem. I will."

Tanner closed his eyes and groaned Josh started licking his sack. It was unbelievable. Sucked off like this? Every night? How lucky could a guy get?

Josh urged Tanner's knees back and to bend, exposing his ass. Tanner's breathing intensified, knowing Josh would most likely spend some time inside his hole. Did he mind? Hell, no.

Never in his life had he felt a climax as intense as the ones Josh gave him. What woman would know how to do that to a man? None he'd encountered.

Josh stopped and stood up. Tanner pouted sadly. "Is something wrong?"

"Nope. Be right back."

Tanner tilted his head to watch. Josh removed something from the nightstand and cupped it to hide it. "Josh?"

"Fear not, sweet damsel."

Tanner laughed. "It's hard not to."

"Hang on."

Waiting nervously, Tanner sighed until Josh's mouth resumed its lovely sucking. As his dick slid into Josh's mouth to his throat, Tanner felt Josh knocking at his back door once again. Grabbing the sheet, Tanner held his breath trying not to shout out, "Stop." Josh hadn't steered him wrong yet.

This time Josh's finger was slick. A cool sensation preempted the penetration. His ring was massaged gently, lovingly, until Tanner relaxed. Josh's fingertip entered his back passage. Tanner was absolutely floored it felt so damn good. "Josh!"

Josh sucked faster, harder, moving his index finger deeper.

"Holy shit!" Tanner thought his cock would burst. He grabbed Josh's head and jammed it against his body, fucking him as hard as he could.

Knowing damn well that Josh's finger was deep inside his ass again, Tanner didn't fucking care. He arched his back and howled in pleasure, thrusting as far as he could reach into Josh's magic mouth. The cum burst out of him in waves of delight. Tanner thought he might pass out.

"Fuck! I am addicted to your fucking mouth!" he cried as the sensations rode on and on and Josh kept milking his cock and stroking inside his ass.

Releasing his grip on Josh's hair, Tanner gasped for breath as he recuperated.

"Now I want your hands." Josh knelt up reaching for Tanner. Josh spread lubrication on himself.

Tanner offered his right hand, completely numb, high from the orgasm, barely aware of what was going on.

Tanner's fingers were trapped in between Josh's as he began fisting his cock.

It took a moment for Tanner to open his eyes and comprehend what Josh was doing. Tanner gazed up at Josh's face as he rose to heights of his own. Soon Josh's back arched and he began to grunt in time with their hands. Tanner's eyes widened in fear as Josh's dick was aimed his way. The cum blew out of Josh's slit and spattered Tanner's pubic hair and thighs.

He blinked in shock and gazed back up at Josh's expression of bliss as his hand was released. "I'm fucking gay. I have to be fucking gay." Tanner gaped in awe as he looked down at the creamy white blobs. "Look at me. I've got a man's spunk on my goddamn pubes."

Josh broke up into demonic laughter and lunged on top of Tanner, smearing his cum all over Tanner's body.

"Josh! You bad boy!" Tanner shouted, breaking up with laughter. "What the hell are you doing to me?'

"Initiating you into the club." Josh laughed with wild abandon. "My spunk on you converts you."

"Shit. Wherever did I find you? You're corrupting me." Tanner wrapped around him with both his arms and his legs, loving the sticky heat that sealed them together.

"If you hold me like this I can slip my dick up your ass," Josh advised.

Suddenly, his heart burning from the power of his climax and his adoration for Josh, Tanner didn't care if he did. He brought Josh to his mouth and kissed him.

Josh grabbed Tanner's face and deepened the kiss to a toe curling, passionate declaration of love.

With his ankles locked behind Josh's hips, Tanner felt Josh's cock dancing between his legs, most likely dying to slip inside his greased hole. And? What if he did? What then?

Wrapping Josh up as tightly as he could, Tanner crushed him in his embrace.

∼

Josh felt his slick cock head resting on the rim of Tanner's ass. It was making him so hot he was dying. The way Tanner was kissing him spoke of affection, attachment. And love?

Unable to stop himself, Josh pressed his hips closer. The top of his dick almost penetrated into Tanner. Josh whimpered in agony, breaking the kiss. Josh clutched Tanner's head to his and cried, "I love you. Tanner, you are an amazing man." Josh reached to the nightstand. "Hang on, hang on." He tore open a rubber and slipped it on his cock as quickly as he could before Tanner could change his mind at what seemed like more experimenting. Instantly Josh was back into his position. "Okay. Keep going."

As if it was possible that Tanner didn't realize what he was doing, Josh felt Tanner tightened his legs, squeezing Josh closer.

Josh wondered what Tanner would do if it happened, because it was about to happen. Josh felt the very tip of the head of his penis dip inside Tanner's anus. "Tanner. Don't tease me. Tanner, Tanner!" Josh began panicking. He wondered if the minute Tanner felt a man's dick in his ass he'd be rejected.

"Just a little so I can see what it's like. Don't pump."

Nodding, stunned, Josh stayed perfectly still. The urge to pound his body into Tanner's was powerful.

"Wow. How bizarre."

"Tanner, *ohmyGod...*" Josh couldn't believe he was allowing him to enter his body like this. It was such a total shock.

"Little more."

Struggling to hold back his tears of joy, Josh inched closer. He released a breath that was mixed with a sob, unable to help it. The sensation of becoming one with his amazing man was overwhelming Josh.

"Unreal. It feels really strange."

"Tanner?" Josh needed reassurance, or he needed to fuck Tanner hard.

Either way he was going completely loco.

"Tiny bit more."

Josh could hardly stand the sensation of being inside him and not pushing up to the hilt.

"Wow...that is mind blowing."

"Want me to pull out?"

"Not yet. Stay still."

Josh was panting, his body breaking out in a sweat. Tanner's arms and legs interlocked so tightly around him he felt like he was in the grasp of a boa constrictor. Tanner tensed his thighs and back passage, increasing the pressure around Josh's cock. Even though he had just come, the sensation of penetrating Tanner was driving him wild. He imagined he was halfway in. "I can't believe you are doing this." The urge Josh had to start hammering his hips was unbearable.

"Me neither. Hang on."

Josh felt Tanner panting for air, his breath on Josh's neck, then his body seemed to release its tension.

"Tiny bit more."

"Oh God, oh God..." Josh sank in deeper. "Tanner, I'm almost all the way inside you."

"Holy shit. I swear, Josh, this is the weirdest feeling in the world. Is this what women feel like?"

"Maybe." Josh tried to control himself. The temptation to begin thrusting inside Tanner was almost beyond his power to control.

"Last push. Slow. Go really slow."

As gingerly as he could, Josh sank his cock all the way into Tanner's ass. He was so stunned he was speechless. Josh imagined this deed to be months off, if ever. How the hell did it happen now?

"Damn. That is fucking amazing."

"You okay?" Josh panted in excitement, wanting Tanner to say, *'Yes, fuck me, babe, give it to me good.'* But that wasn't going to happen.

"Just stay still. Don't pump, please."

"All right." Josh closed his eyes, feeling Tanner's body throb against his cock. "Jesus, Tanner. It feels like heaven."

"Yeah?"

"Yeah."

"It's strange. It's like nothing I've ever imagined."

Josh laughed softly as the tears ran down his cheeks.

"Okay. Pull out."

As gently as he could, Josh removed himself from Tanner's body. He sat back on his heels and stared at Tanner in awe. "You are unreal."

"Are you crying?"

"Yes." Josh tugged off the condom and dropped it over the side of the bed.

"Josh..." Tanner sat up and hugged him. "Don't cry."

"I'm so floored you did that."

"Well, your dick was right there. And you had me lubed like an old '67 Chevy Impala."

Josh laughed and more tears fell from his eyes. "Did you like it?"

"I'm not sure." Tanner sat back. "I guess I was just curious."

"Yes." Josh wiped at his tears with his knuckles. "We already came. So, I imagine it would feel a hell of a lot better if you needed to. A whole lot better." Josh grinned wickedly at him.

"I know. I did think of that. But, I just wanted to test the waters. It does feel great when you put your finger in there. I never knew I had a come button."

Josh laughed again, crying at the same time. "Tanner, I love exploring with you."

Tanner tousled Josh's hair playfully. "You're like a new jungle gym for me to climb on."

"Man," Josh announced, "you said a mouthful."

"We should eat some dinner."

"Yes. We should." Josh paused and held Tanner back. "I love you so much, Tanner."

Tanner kissed him. "You're such a sweetheart."

Smiling at him, Josh watched as he walked to the bathroom to wash up. Dabbing at his eyes, Josh couldn't get over what Tanner allowed him to do and he knew every time he thought about it, he would tear up and cry.

᛫᛫᛫

Tanner sat at the kitchen table, munching on a mushroom pizza they had delivered. He kept getting flutters in his stomach at having allowed Josh to penetrate him. Now, cleaned up, clothed, and eating dinner together, Tanner wondered what got into him to experiment like that. It wasn't like him. Not at all.

Glancing up at Josh while he chewed his pizza, Tanner met his shy gaze and returned his smile.

"You okay, Tanner?"

"Huh? Yes. I'm okay."

"It's intense, isn't it?"

"Very. I keep feeling like I'm way out of my comfort zone." Tanner finished his crust and brushed his hands off.

"I can imagine. I remember the first time I had anal sex."

"High school?"

"Yup. Tom Ryder. Captain of the football team."

"Yeah?" Tanner laughed, reaching for another piece of pie from the cardboard box.

Josh held the lid up for him. "Yeah. What a stud."

"Thanks." Tanner laid the slice on his plate and took a sip of beer. "So? What was it like?"

"I think it hurt. Yes. It hurt. We didn't have lube. He spit on his dick and went at it."

"Ouch. That doesn't sound very comfortable." Tanner wriggled on the chair pad. He did not feel any residual effects from the little foray they'd had.

"It wasn't. But I let him do it anyway."

Tanner swallowed first, asking, "Why?"

Josh shrugged. "He wanted to. And I suppose I liked him and didn't want him to ignore me. I was afraid if I didn't let him do it, he'd never hang out with me again."

"Josh, that doesn't sound like a very nice first experience." Tanner grew upset with the story.

"I suppose not. But I felt like I was the school freak or something, Tanner. All the other boys dated girls. I just couldn't force myself to do it. One day, after football practice, Tom and I were walking home together. We'd always been sort of friends. You know, we were on the same team and we had a few classes in common. I think he knew I had a crush on him and was leaning toward being gay. We cut through a field on the way home. He tackled me, yanked my jeans down my ass and took my virginity."

Tanner stopped chewing and stared at him. "Josh, that sounds like he forced you."

"No. Not really. I could have stopped him. I just didn't."

Tanner pictured the scene a little too well.

"The only problem was he told the rest of the guys about it. He said I was an easy lay."

Tanner paused, waiting for something more though he had a feeling he didn't want to hear it.

"I had the boys pestering me constantly after that." Josh set his crust down and wiped his hands and mouth. "The teasing was a little merciless. Once two of the bigger boys pinned me to the gym locker making all sorts of lewd comments about what they wanted to do to me. They never did. I knew it was bravado. I only gave Tom the rights to my ass."

"Did you get to screw him?"

"Hell no. He didn't even let me kiss him."

"What? That doesn't sound very fair." Tanner sipped more of his ale.

Josh shrugged. "I was sixteen. What the hell did I know?"

"So, you just let his Tom guy have you anytime he wanted you?"

"Pretty much." Josh took another bite of his crust, staring at Tanner.

"And what about the guy you met in college?"

"You mean my roommate? Gavin Wallace?"

"Is he the one you went out with in college?" Tanner ate more of his pizza.

"I don't think we were really going out." Josh relaxed in his chair and brought his beer to his lips.

"I thought you said you had a boyfriend in college."

"I wouldn't qualify him as a real boyfriend. Not like by boy-meets-girl standards."

Tanner was growing more concerned by the minute. "Was it like the relationship you had with Tom?"

"I'm afraid so."

"Joshua!"

"What?" Josh reacted, wincing.

"Why do you just let guys use you?"

"Did I do that?"

Tanner glared at him in annoyance. "Did he love you?"

"I doubt it. He never said he did. I got the impression he was bi-curious."

"He just got to fuck you?" Tanner responded.

"Yes."

"Jesus, Josh...you're too good to be treated like that."

"Am I?" Josh seemed to find that amusing. "How so?"

Tanner finished his slice and wiped his hands and mouth with a napkin. "How so? You shouldn't just let guys who don't really like you have their way with you."

"I didn't hate it. I got to be with them on an intimate level. What was I supposed to do? I needed the affection, Tanner. I crave being accepted and liked."

"Everyone does, but you don't have to allow men to use you like that in order to be accepted." Tanner dropped his napkin on his plate. "Don't do that anymore."

"Are you joking? I'm doing it with you."

Tanner felt pale. *Was he? Was Josh being used sexually in this relationship?*

Josh leaned closer, touching Tanner's arm. Tanner woke from his thoughts.

"Look, Tanner, I realize you'll never be able to give me the stability of a committed relationship. I'm not an idiot. I know this is some passing fancy on your part while you're in between women. I wish it weren't that way, but I'm not so naïve that I believe you'll fall madly in love with me and declare it to the world." Josh clasped Tanner's hand. "You and I will have some physical fun together and you will move on. It's already happened three times to me in the only three relationships I've ever had."

Tanner felt like the worst heel. His cheeks grew warm as he realized the truth in that sentiment. What were the chances he'd ever grow comfortable in a same sex relationship?

"And I am so grateful to you already, Tanner."

Tanner met his eyes.

"You are the first one to allow me to penetrate their bodies."

"What?" Tanner blinked in surprise.

"Yes. Even Luis, the man I met at Buzzworks. He did the screwing, Tanner. Not me." Josh lowered his eyes shyly. "And even that wasn't enough. He cheated on me as well. I can't seem to find anything real. I end up giving my heart only to see it trampled." Josh raised his eyelashes again, revealing his green irises. "It's my lot."

Tanner lunged out of his chair and wrapped his arms around Josh, embracing him. Tanner brought Josh to his feet, squeezing him closer. "No. I won't do that to you."

A soft laugh reached Tanner's ears. "You will, Tanner. You will."

Crushing Josh to his chest, Tanner closed his eyes, hating the fact that he could be that cruel to such a wonderful man. But could he?

Was he truly ready to pack in his other life? The life of a straight man and take the plunge into gay living?

Maybe Josh knew something he didn't. But the notion that he would eventually stomp Josh's heart, terrified him.

"Are you done eating?"

Tanner set back to see Josh's face at the cold comment. Affectionately, Tanner brushed Josh's hair back from his eyes. "Joshua, look at me."

Those nervous green eyes slowly obeyed.

"I will never set out intentionally to harm you. Or to use you."

"No one ever does." Josh's smile was full of pain. "But the end result is always the same. Maybe I just make bad choices. I don't know."

"Leave the plates for a minute." Tanner brought Josh to the sofa, sitting him down on it with him. Taking both of Josh's hands into his, Tanner kissed his knuckles, running his mouth over them.

"The guilt got to you?" Josh smiled ironically. "I didn't say those things to make you feel bad, Tanner."

Pressing Josh's hands to his chest, Tanner replied, "A part of me wants to pursue this to the dire end."

"Which part? Your dick or your heart?"

"Both." Tanner tried to smile but there really wasn't anything funny about it.

"And what is your definition of 'the dire end'?"

"Us. Living together."

"What?" Josh gasped.

"Calm down. You see, this is part of the problem I have with you. Your fuse is lit again and soon the big bang will follow. Slow down."

"Slow down?" Josh laughed at the absurdity. "You just dropped the bomb, not me."

"Josh...please."

Josh paid attention.

"I do realize there are a lot of benefits to having a monogamous relationship with you. A man."

"Yeah?" Josh appeared intrigued.

"Yes. If you don't think I've thought about it night after sleepless night. Think again."

"Tell me. What are the benefits?"

"Stop looking so damn amused." Tanner pecked his lips.

"I'll try. Tell me."

Tanner took a deep breath. "As you know, I don't want children. For some reason, almost all the young ladies out there in the world do. I assume it's some Mother Nature thing that I'll never understand. But saying that, you and I don't have that particular monumental problem." Tanner waited for Josh to say something. He didn't, waiting patiently for more.

"Also…" Tanner tightened his hold on Josh's fingers. "The sex thing. Another problem I've encountered with women is their drive seems to be low. Or at least lower than mine. Again, something we don't have to deal with." Tanner almost melted from the gaze of adoration he was receiving from Josh. Trying to keep a clear head, Tanner kept going. "It's been my experience that a good man is hard working, lends a hand to the finances, the odd jobs around the house, likes to drink on occasion, enjoys sports…" Tanner asked, "You like sports?"

"Yup."

Nodding, Tanner resumed, "Men tend to overlap on most things. I'm not interested in shopping malls, ballet, big catered affairs… Am I right?"

"Correct." Josh smiled.

"Good. So the eternal rub is that men and women are expected to somehow cohabitate and get along even though they have nothing in common. Still with me?"

"I am. With you all the way, Tanner."

"Now we're back to the problems I see in accepting this alternate lifestyle."

"No. Do we have to go there? Can't we rehash all the positives again? Then maybe crawl into bed to celebrate them?"

"Christ, you are so damn adorable." Tanner kissed him. "No. Let me finish."

"But I already know the routine, Tanner. But…but…you don't want people to know your butt is gay."

Tanner bit his lip. Yes, that was the only drawback. And shit, what a whopper it was.

Josh smiled knowingly. "Shut you up, didn't it?"

"Josh…"

"Tanner…your turn."

"Stop."

"Tanner, if I can't laugh about it, I'll cry."

Feeling so sorry for putting Josh through this, Tanner cupped his jaw and brought him to his mouth. When their lips touched, it didn't feel strange, awkward, or different. It was Josh. That was all.

*

Josh dug his hands into Tanner's thick, brown hair. The contact was sizzling in its passion. Knowing one day he would have to say goodbye, Josh felt emotional once more. Why? Why did he have to let Tanner go? Couldn't someone stick around for him? Love him enough to make him feel worth something?

Josh's eyes opened wide in astonishment when Tanner's hands slipped into his shorts from behind, smoothing down his bottom. Another first.

Instantly, Josh's cock surged with pleasure and the kissing grew even more frantic.

Josh's ass cheeks were kneaded with strong, deep rubbing fingers. It made Josh groan in yearning, which began in his crotch and worked its way to his throat.

A finger slid down Josh's crack. It made Josh push hard against Tanner's engorged cock. It felt so natural, Josh wondered if he was dreaming.

Josh broke the kiss so he could take a deep inhalation of air.

"Come back to bed," Tanner said.

A catch formed in Josh's throat. He almost asked why? *Stupid me!*

Josh's ass was squeezed again. Tanner removed his hands and held one of Josh's, escorting him to the bedroom. Too stunned to react, Josh waited for Tanner to lead.

Josh waited as Tanner, dressed only in his red swimsuit, splayed out on the bed, reaching out to him. Josh crawled on his hands and knees and met Tanner in the middle. He was urged to lie next to Tanner and they ended up on their sides, facing each other like mirror images.

Josh's hair was caressed gently. Tanner stared at him with unmatched intensity. Try as he might, Josh couldn't stop panting hard from his excitement.

A long moment passed where nothing was said but everything was implied. Josh didn't want to love him more, but he just couldn't help it.

Josh felt his skin shiver with chills when Tanner touched him. He watched Tanner explore his body, something he had never expected Tanner to want to do.

With the very tips of his fingers, Tanner began at Josh's neck and delicately made his way around Josh's chest. His nipples were brushed over until they were hard little nubs. The excitement at having Tanner stimulate them drove Josh insane.

Josh was delirious while Tanner spent some time moving from one to the other, circling around like his digits were planets and Josh's nipples were suns. Once Tanner made a move downward, Josh labored for breath he was so hot. Though he wanted to touch Tanner, he kept his hands still.

With his knuckles, Tanner ran over the ripples of Josh's abdominal muscles. As he grazed by Josh's belly button and the hair leading to his pelvis, Josh shivered.

Finally, Tanner dipped his fingers past the elastic waistband of Josh's red swimsuit. Josh held his breath as Tanner ran into the head of his erection. He peeled the fabric back, exposing it. Josh moaned in longing.

Once again, using the back of his fingers, Tanner brushed against the tip. Josh noticed the shiny drops of his pre-cum glistening on Tanner's hands.

"Tanner..." Josh was slowly moving toward agony.

Tanner nudged him, toppling Josh over onto his back. "Take these off."

Josh closed his eyes to stop his head from spinning at the request. He raised his hips and peeled his suit off, pushing it onto the floor.

❦

*How could anyone abuse this man?*

Tanner took a moment to gaze at Josh from head to toe. Josh's nude body wasn't making him uncomfortable any longer. Maybe seeing it a few times, hugging him, kissing him, had made Tanner more at ease.

It was wrong to keep taking. It was criminal.

Imagining callous men receiving their pleasure from Josh and giving him nothing in return angered Tanner to the point of fury.

Tanner looked up at Josh's face. Josh seemed so unsure of himself and frightened, not the confident flirt at all. Just a scared little boy. It was very different than the first impression Tanner had from him on the day they met.

Using his knuckles again, Tanner ran his hand down Josh's side. It felt like satin. Tanner brushed over Josh's hip, tracing the line that separated his external oblique from his stomach muscles. Tanner found his hand back at Josh's penis.

*It's just a cock, Tanner. You've got one, remember? How different could it feel to your own?*

Not just a cock. Josh Elliot's cock.

Tanner petted it with a light upstroke of his fingertips. It reacted like a cat and elevated to meet them. Teasing it lightly, he was fascinated by its size, its heat, the vein running along the length underneath to the neatly proportioned head. It bobbed and seeped, connecting a string of pre-cum between the slit and Josh's body.

Tanner glanced up at Josh's face again. His eyes had closed and his lips parted.

Tanner closed his fingers around Josh's length, feeling it throb and seeing it ooze more fluid. It made Tanner's own cock pulsate in his swimsuit.

Josh raised his leg, bending at the knee to open up access to his body.

Using his thumb, Tanner rubbed over the slit, feeling the velvety softness and the sticky, slick drops. Josh moaned, his hips elevating slightly.

It wasn't horrible touching Josh this way, seeing Josh's pleasure, his joy, knowing exactly how this felt for him. And the added bonus was his own delight, his own prick beating down the door of the fabric it was trapped under.

*Maybe you are gay, Tanner. This isn't half-bad.*

Tanner smoothed his palm down Josh's shaft to his balls. The whimpers coming from Josh were exquisite. Wrapping his hand around his sack, feeling it tense up and then soften with his caresses, Tanner glanced back at Josh's face to see his bliss.

Tanner sat up next to him and continued to fondle Josh's testicles with his right hand, reaching for his shaft with his left. Tanner worked his two hands in tandem. Josh began to writhe on the bed. Tanner knew what he liked while he masturbated and assumed most men would be partial to the same until he was told differently. He squeezed tighter on the upstroke while rubbing his fingers on the root of Josh's cock, close to his anus. More fluid leaked out and Josh's hips began to rock.

Tanner looked forward to making Josh come, licking his lips in anticipation, he increased his speed and pushed dangerously close to Josh's puckered rim.

"Tanner...Tanner..." Josh gasped in breathy bursts.

In Tanner's palm, Josh's cock hardened to stone and began throbbing. Tanner pressed his index finger into Josh's hole the way Josh had done to him. Cream erupted from Josh's prick as he arched his back and whimpered in ecstasy.

The satisfaction Tanner felt at giving Josh a climax was unexpected. Slowing down his hand, running over the tip of Josh's cock to feel his cum, Tanner stroked his balls lovingly as he recuperated. Releasing his hold on Josh's body,

Tanner gazed down at his sticky fingers. He rubbed his thumb over the other four fingertips in awe of the lubrication between them. He caught Josh's amazed stare. As Josh looked on, Tanner brought one of his fingers to his lips to taste.

"Holy shit." Josh was riveted to Tanner's actions.

Tanner licked his finger curiously. It was tangy, slightly salty. Tanner peeked down at his own crotch. The sight of a stain saturating his suit astounded him.

As if on springs, Josh sat up, grabbed Tanner's hand and sucked Tanner's fingers into his mouth, one by one. The emotion Tanner felt at the gesture staggered him. Was he falling in love with this wonderful man?

*Am I gay?*

Tanner fell back on the bed at Josh's urgent push. Tanner regained his wits. Josh was sucking on the wet spot in his swimsuit. Shivering down to his toes, Tanner moaned in disbelief.

His stiff cock was soon flipped out of his shorts and they were very efficiently removed. Then that hot mouth was on him again. Jesus, how he loved Josh's mouth!

Tanner wasn't sure what hit him. He was slapped senseless by this gorgeous god who was king of the art of fellatio.

In no time Tanner was on the verge, clutching the bed under him and tensing his muscles for the blast. Choking at the intensity, the churning at the root of his cock and balls, Tanner couldn't believe what he was feeling. As if Josh was propelling him into outer orbit, Tanner came, thrusting his pelvis up into Josh's mouth. Once again, he grabbed Josh's head to deepen the penetration and pressed as hard as he could into him. He couldn't prevent it. With Josh, he became an animal who simply couldn't come hard enough.

It lasted so long Tanner imagined emptying the contents of his balls. Once it finally began to subside, he rested his hand on his chest to feel the thunder of his heart rate. His cock still being licked and mouthed gently, Tanner tried to come back to earth, but struggled.

Josh nestled beside him, into his neck and purred happily.

"Josh…never in my wildest dreams…"

"Mm." Josh rubbed his hair against Tanner's, rumbling with more purring sounds.

"Joshua, Joshua, Joshua…"

"Tanner, Tanner, Tanner…your turn."

Laughing, Tanner echoed, "Joshua, Joshua, Joshua!"

Josh leapt on top of him and wriggled as he exclaimed, "Tanner! Tanner! Tanner!"

"Get over here." Tanner trapped Josh's face and kissed him, tasting his own cum on Josh's tongue in awe.

After a good, long smooch, Josh smiled at him. "Do you love me yet?"

"Close. Oh, pretty baby, very, very close." Tanner pushed Josh's hair back from his dewy forehead.

"Good. Very good." Josh snaked his arms around Tanner's back and kissed him again.

# Chapter Eleven

A boiling hot Friday afternoon set the stage for a packed beach. As the days of brilliant summer weather continued, the sand became a patchwork quilt of blankets, towels, and bamboo mats in a rainbow of colors. Children screamed and ran from the surf's rushing foam, students strutted their stuff as their school year finished, and the lifeguards were busy watching everyone and everything.

Josh held the binoculars to his eyes while on the tower. Feeling a warm body next to him, Josh turned toward Tanner who had joined him, leaning on the rail to have a look around. Josh smiled adoringly at him and moved close enough to brush Tanner's arm, putting the binoculars back to his eyes.

"What's going on over there, Josh?" Tanner nudged him and pointed.

Josh shifted his vision to the direction suggested. "I can't tell. Here." Josh handed him the binoculars and flipped his sunglasses down to block the glare.

Josh waited as Tanner surveyed the scene, becoming concerned. "What do you see, Tanner?" Josh asked, still trying to determine where the problem was.

Tanner stuck his whistle in his mouth, sending out two blasts, then he picked up a rescue can and raised it over his head.

Josh noticed Destiny and Samantha in the next tower wave they had seen him.

Tanner gestured to the direction. The women took off running. The whistle dropped out of Tanner's mouth. "I see a small crowd gathering. That usually means someone's down."

Josh took back the binoculars. He followed the women's progress and did indeed see a small circle of people. "You're awesome."

"Just experience, Josh."

They waited for a moment, looking for a signal from the women to see if they needed help.

Destiny waved at them in what Josh interpreted as the all's okay sign.

Josh looked back at the water again and scanned the bobbing bathers, making sure everyone appeared after dunking under the waves.

Josh turned to meet Tanner's smile when Tanner touched his back. It was just a gentle brush of his hand, but it meant everything to Josh.

"When Destiny and Samantha get back to their tower, I want you to walk the beach."

"Okay," Josh replied, resisting the urge to wriggle against him adoringly.

Ten minutes later the women were back at their tower, Tanner brushed his hand through Josh's hair affectionately. "Take a can with you."

Josh reached for one, looking out at the thick mob of people. He felt like a speck of sand on the overcrowded beach. It didn't seem possible that so few guards could keep so many people safe.

---

Tanner noticed Destiny jogging in his direction.

She met him and stood beside the tower. "That incident was just a guy choking on his sandwich."

"You didn't have to run all the way here to tell me that."

"I wanted to get some exercise anyway." She looked off in the direction Josh had taken. "Where's Mr. Perfect going?"

"Mr. Perfect? What's with the attitude?" Tanner asked.

"What attitude?"

"Destiny, cut it out."

She threw up her hands. "I can't believe you asked for him to be assigned with you. Now you have your little favorite, Mr. Perfect Josh Elliot by your side."

Tanner stared at her in disbelief. "What's brought this on?"

"Why did you ask him to work with you? You know Samantha and I have been lifeguards a hell of a lot longer than he has. Or was it something else, Tanner? Huh?"

Tanner's anger grew. "I thought Josh was top notch in his skills and he could benefit from working with an experienced permanent."

A choking sound was his reply.

"Destiny. What's really going on?" Tanner had a feeling he already knew and dreaded it.

She finally met his gaze. "You like him, don't you?"

"Of course I like him. Why shouldn't I?"

"No. I mean, *like* him."

Tanner stiffened his back and didn't answer the overt accusation.

"Tanner, the guy is extremely gay. Everyone knows it. Okay? You know how that looks? Huh? You and he working together after mentoring?"

"Yes. So? Do I have to send you to a refresher course on diversity?"

"Sure. Punish me. I expect it."

"Expect it?" Tanner was lost.

"Yes. Go ahead. Make a formal complaint."

"Where the hell is all this coming from? Josh has only been here a week and you're becoming unhinged."

"Unhinged? Screw you, Tanner." She gave him the finger and started heading back to her tower.

He raced down to stop her. "Will you level with me and tell me what the hell is really on your mind?"

"I'm jealous, okay?"

"Jealous?" He felt his stomach go cold, but he'd expected as much.

"You know I want to go out with you. I've only asked you a million times to have a drink after work. But who do you request to work with, Tanner? And I know he always waits for you after shift."

They'd been seen. Well, it wasn't rocket science.

"I do enjoy his company, Destiny. I won't deny that. But it's not what you're thinking."

"What am I thinking?" She crossed her arms defensively as she settled her weight on one leg.

Was this how it was going to be? He and Josh seen socializing and suddenly every woman who had designs on him was going to make him answer to them?

"Just go back to your tower. It's too busy to get into this discussion and, to be honest, I don't want to even have it." He couldn't, and shouldn't have to, defend his actions.

With another grumble in disgust, Destiny walked away.

Tanner shook off the effect of the terrible conversation. He tried to find Josh, putting the binoculars to his eyes, scanning the beach. He promptly realized Nathan and Josh were in the water, performing a rescue.

His adrenalin kicking in, Tanner raced to the hut, grabbed his medical backpack and took off across the sand.

Josh had the buoy in his hand, swimming with the victim to the shore. A crowd had gathered to gape. He held the young man around the chest. The man wasn't responding to his commands but he was alert and conscious.

Josh dreaded a scene and the hysterics that might go with it. He found his footing and Nathan stepped up and supported the limp swimmer from the opposite side. The moment Josh could, he set the man down on the sand and had a look at him. He had a gash on his lower leg that was bleeding heavily.

"Get Tanner!" Josh shouted to Nathan who looked pure white from the sight.

Without another word, Nathan rushed to a clearing in the mob, holding the buoy over his head in a distress signal.

"A towel! Does anyone have a towel I can use?" Josh gazed up at the dumbfounded spectators. Someone tossed him one. He pressed it against the young man's leg, elevating it as high as he could. Josh had no idea how the man could have cut himself so badly in the surf. Seeing the man's eyes flutter, Josh rubbed his arm. "You with me, buddy?"

"What happened?"

"You have a cut on your leg. Lay still. Help is coming."

"Am I bleeding?"

Josh looked back at the soaked towel. "Uh, a little. Just rest." *Come on, Tanner! Come on.*

At a noise behind him, Josh could see Tanner shoving the growing crowd aside. "All right, get back! Josh?"

"Tanner. He's cut."

Taking off his backpack, Tanner went to work quickly on getting the slice closed and covered. "He needs stitches." Tanner ordered him, "Signal the next tower to call 911."

Josh jumped up and held the buoy over his head, hoping the next tower was watching him. Seeing an acknowledgement, Josh turned his attention back to the young man. "How you doing? Holding out?"

"Yes. How did I cut myself?"

"I don't know. You tell me." Josh smiled at him, reaching to hold his hand.

The young man gripped it tightly. "All I remember was getting smashed by a wave and hitting the sand."

"Ah. Then my guess is it was a piece of glass."

"As long as it wasn't a shark."

"No, judging by the look of it, I doubt it was a shark."

Once he stabilized the bleeding, Tanner wrapped a BP cuff around the young man's arm. "You doing okay?"

"So far." The man smiled bravely.

"Where's Nat?" Josh looked around. It was then he noticed another little crowd adjacent to theirs.

A woman hurried toward him and Tanner. "I'm afraid one of your fellow lifeguards has passed out."

Josh met Tanner's eye and held back his laugh. It wasn't really funny, was it? Nathan fainting at the sight of blood?

"Can you sit him up and put his head between his knees for me?" Tanner was all business at the moment.

The woman rushed to do as he asked. Tanner caught Josh's eyes, shaking his head.

The sound of a chirping siren was heard, making its way closer. Josh strained to look over the gawkers to see the rescue truck and two familiar faces. "Our firemen are back."

Tanner twisted over his shoulder, yelling at the growing crowd, "Let them through!"

Hunter and Blake rushed between the parted throng and knelt down next to Tanner.

"He's got a laceration down his left shin. Pulse is one hundred BPM and BP one forty over ninety. Conscious and alert." Tanner asked the man, "How old are you?"

"Nineteen."

Hunter took a look at the bandage that was already seeping. "We'll get the board. Better keep him horizontal and that leg elevated."

"Okay. Josh, go check on Nathan."

Stifling his smile, Josh released the young man's hand and hurried to his co-worker. Seeing Nathan's pale, sweaty face and a few people hovering around him, Josh knelt down by him and touched his cheek. "Are you going to live?"

"Yeah. How embarrassing."

"The sight of blood. It does it to some people." Josh touched Nathan's forehead and could feel the sweat on him.

"Is the guy okay?"

"Yes. The fire department is here. They're taking him to the hospital for stitches.

"Oh."

"Can you stand?"

"I think so."

Josh rose up and reached out his hand. He hauled Nathan to his feet, placed his arm around his waist and brought him back to Tanner.

They found the two firemen and Tanner securing the long board to the truck. Josh released Nathan and walked to the young man. Josh's hand was grasped when he offered it. "You still alive?" Josh smiled.

"Yeah. Thanks. I owe you."

"You don't owe me. I'm just doing my job." Josh pushed the young man's hair back from his eyes. "You'll be okay. You're in good hands now." He tilted his head at the two handsome medics.

Hunter stood next to Josh once he was done strapping the board down. "How are you doing? All better now?"

"I'm raring to go." Josh gave him a big smile. "What is it about firemen?"

"Down boy." Hunter grinned playfully.

"Is he causing trouble again?" Blake shouted as he opened the driver's side door. "Tanner, put a leash on him, will ya?"

"That's easier said than done." Tanner's light eyes gleamed.

The young man's hand squeezed his. Josh looked down at him.

"Are you gay?"

Josh blushed and leaned closer to whisper in his ear, "Yes."

"Single?"

"No." Josh winked at him affectionately.

"Too bad."

"Are you flirting again?" Hunter gasped. "We have to get this young man to the hospital for stitches."

"Go!" Josh released the man's hand. "Good luck to you."

"See you around?"

"I'll be here," Josh replied. "Goodbye, gentlemen. Always a pleasure seeing you." Josh waved to the two medics.

"You too, Josh, you too." Hunter waved back as they left, the siren chirping to get people out of their way.

Josh turned around, finding Tanner putting his things back into his backpack. He crouched down to help him.

"You did very well, Josh. What can I say? You're a natural."

"Thanks, Tanner."

They both looked up and found Nathan appearing shy and embarrassed.

"You, on the other hand..." Tanner sighed, throwing his kit over his shoulder. "We have to get you acclimated to the sight of blood."

"I'm sorry. It just got to me. It won't happen again."

Tanner put his arm around Nathan's shoulders. "You'll get used to it. Thanks for the assist."

"No problem. See ya." Nathan headed to his tower.

Josh picked up his rescue buoy, winding the lead back up around it. He fell in behind Tanner, watching his hips as they swayed hypnotically.

Tanner noticed and paused allowing Josh to catch up. "Walk with me, hero."

Josh smiled sweetly at him.

Destiny was at their tower again. "You guys get everything under control?"

"Yes. Thank you." Tanner passed her by to enter the hut.

Josh hung the rescue can on the rail. About to go into the hut for his bottle of water, he noticed Destiny glaring at him. "What?"

"I can't believe you're gay." Destiny stared at his crotch.

"Why can't you believe it?"

"It's such a waste."

"Trust me. It's not wasted." Josh waited until she stormed off. He found Tanner at the counter, updating the log sheet. Once Josh had located his bottle of water, he paused to stare at Tanner.

"So?" Tanner gave Josh his attention. "Talk to me about the rescue."

"I noticed him get slammed by a wave. He went right down and he came up screaming."

"Oh." Tanner chuckled. "I guess that would make you sit up and take notice."

"I ran in and tried to get him to hold the can but he was too freaked out. He thought a shark had gotten him."

"Yes. That is the normal reaction. Thank *Jaws* for that."

"My guess is he got whacked to the sand and a piece of bottle glass cut him."

"That would be my guess as well. Did you get his zip code by any chance?"

"Shit, no Tanner. I forgot to ask him. Sorry."

"No big deal."

As they returned to the front of the tower to keep watch, Josh asked, "Are you coming over tonight?"

"You want me to?"

"Mm." Josh rubbed his own cock in a tease.

His blue eyes glittering in the sun, Tanner shook his head. "You got it, naughty boy."

Josh approached him, running his hand through Tanner's hair softly. Tanner's eyes darted behind him. Josh pulled back and spun around.

Destiny was there, watching them. "I knew it."

Josh died inside. "Knew what?" he confronted her.

"Why are you still here?" Tanner accused. "You know damn well you should be back at your own tower with Samantha."

"Yeah, Destiny," Josh echoed. "Go back to your own hut."

"Cut it out, Josh. Everyone can see what's going on with you two."

"That's enough," Tanner chided. "Leave."

"Fine." As she walked off both men could hear her mutter, "Asshole."

"Sorry, Tanner." Josh knew it was worse for him.

"Don't worry. She's been looking for a reason to hate me ever since I passed on her advances." Tanner sighed. "My luck she'll spread gossip behind our backs."

"Do you want to talk with her? Try and smooth things out?" Josh asked meekly.

"Are you offering?" Tanner grinned impishly.

"Grrr." Josh curled his lip in revulsion. "I'll only do it for you. Believe me, gossip doesn't scare me like it used to. But I do worry for your reputation. Er... do I really have to?"

Tanner cracked a smile.

"I'll only talk to her if we get together tonight."

"I already said yes, didn't I? Your place?"

"Great. Bring your toothbrush."

"Why?"

"You're staying over."

"Am I?" Tanner acted shocked.

"Yes. That's an order."

"I knew the day was near when my subordinates would begin bossing me around."

"Yup. Too bad."

Tanner smiled at him, shaking his head.

※

Later that afternoon, Josh noticed Destiny walking by herself down the beach. Josh was nudged by Tanner. Josh rolled his eyes and tacitly agreed jogging to meet up with her. As he approached her, her expression darkened.

"Hey."

"What do you want?" She looked back at her tower.

"You waiting for someone?" Josh looked around.

"Yes. Sam and I were going to patrol the beach."

"Oh? You two close?" Josh teased.

She sneered in reply.

"Gee, you mean just because you and Samantha like one another you're not lesbians? How could that be?"

"Shut up. You already announced you were gay, stop acting like a jerk."

"Just because I'm gay doesn't mean everyone I'm fond of is sticking their dick up my ass."

"Ew. You're gross." She crossed her arms over her chest. "I can tell Tanner likes you."

"So? Can't one gay guy and one straight guy like each other? Is there a law against it? I didn't remember learning that in the academy."

"Why do you keep denying you're hot for Tanner?"

"Why do *you* keep denying it?" Josh echoed.

Destiny sighed, looking back for Samantha anxiously.

Josh did the same, making sure no one was coming or could overhear them.

"I know what this is about. Just because you're not Tanner's type you're lashing out at him."

"What are you? A shrink?"

"No. But I'm not stupid either. It's hard to get rejected, isn't it?"

"Shut up."

"Look, Destiny, we have to work together. Can't we just call a truce or something? Does there have to be animosity between us?"

"I don't like you. Okay? You're a conceited jerk."

"A conceited jerk?" Josh shook his head. "Why do I feel like I'm back in grammar school?" Seeing he had reached a dead end, he threw up his hands. "I tried. It's not my fault you're pigheaded."

"Get lost." She twisted away from him.

In a daze, thinking about their conversation, Josh returned to the tower only to find it was vacant. He felt a slight flutter of worry, but tried to keep calm. Stepping up to the rail, Josh used the binoculars to search for Tanner.

An inflatable rescue boat was in the water by an overturned kayak. The crewmember on board was equipped with a helmet and lifejacket. Josh could not find Tanner.

"Fuck this." Josh grabbed a rescue can and started running toward the action. He felt anxious and needed to see Tanner. Where the hell was he?

As he sprinted across the hot sand, someone raced after him, shouting for his help. Halting in his tracks, Josh spun around, upset that he had to make a detour. If he didn't find out where Tanner was, he'd lose it.

"My son is sick. Please."

Nodding, Josh hurried to where the woman led him. There on a blanket under an umbrella was an infant. Josh tossed the buoy aside and asked, "What's wrong?"

"He's throwing up. I don't know why." She wrung her hands and fell to her knees beside Josh.

"He's overheated." Josh picked the child up in his arms and walked him down to the water. He knew anything associated with infants was bad news. Scanning the water, looking at that IRB and trying not to be distracted, Josh crouched down by the water and wet his hands, attempting to cool the child off. "He needs medical care. I don't like to take any chances with a child this tiny."

Josh took off the little cotton cap the baby wore, soaked it in the water and placed it back on his head. "Come on. I need to take him back to the tower so I can use the emergency line." He rushed to grab his rescue can and hurried with the child in his arms, the frantic mother behind him. All the while he was dying inside at not knowing where Tanner was.

Josh gave the mother back the baby and picked up the phone, dialing 911. "I have an infant, uh…how old?" Josh asked the woman.

"Nine months."

"A nine month old infant apparently suffering heatstroke or overheated. I've tried to cool him down, but I thought he should get medical help."

"Vitals?"

Josh paused. "Ah, conscious, not alert, uh…" He reached for the child's hand and couldn't feel a pulse easily. "Crap." He got back on the phone. "I can't find a pulse at the moment, but he's breathing, not labored."

"Help is on the way."

Josh tried to feel the child's heartbeat at his neck, then his leg, giving up because he couldn't focus he was so worried about Tanner. "Sit down," he told the woman and helped her to a chair, checking on the baby again in agony. He paced, chewed his lip, rubbed his forehead in anxiety, and wished the medics would show up so he could get back out there and find Tanner.

Josh heard a truck engine and dashed to the front of the tower. "In here." He followed two EMTs he did not know inside the hut as they crouched down to examine the baby. Josh wanted to say, "You got it? Good," and run back to the beach, but instead he sat tight.

*Tanner, Tanner…if anything happens to you, I'll die.*

The medics conferred.

"Let's take him in to the ER to be sure."

"Yeah, that's my opinion as well."

Josh shifted his weight impatiently as the medics escorted the woman out to their truck.

"We're taking the baby to the emergency room to be on the safe side."

"Yes. Of course." Josh nodded to them.

"Good call."

"Thanks." Josh waited as they loaded the baby into a car seat with his mother by his side. Once the truck was on its way, Josh looked back at the sea. The inflatable rescue boat was gone.

"Where the hell is everyone?" The beach was so packed, Josh felt overwhelmed. And it wasn't even July fourth yet. He was floored that so few staff had to take care of a crowd so huge.

"Tanner," he whined in frustration. "Where the hell are you?"

He couldn't stand there any longer. It was making him anxious. Grabbing a can, Josh took off running down the beach again, looking for someone, anyone.

Along the way, he kept being distracted. People complaining to him about loud music, open containers of alcohol, obnoxious people annoying other obnoxious people, it was enough to drive him crazy. Suddenly Josh felt as if he was completely alone and left to deal with ten thousand inmates in an insane asylum.

Finally, he noticed Nathan walking back to his tower. Josh raced toward him, relieved someone else finally materialized. "Nat!"

He spun around appearing completely exhausted.

"Nat, where's Tanner?"

"He's been taken to the hospital, Josh."

Josh felt like passing out. He must have looked like it because Nathan grabbed his arm quickly and led him to the ramp to sit down.

"No." Josh tried to catch his breath. "Why? What happened?"

"A kayak capsized and the man couldn't manage to get upright or out." Nathan continued, "Tanner and I rushed out to help the guy. He nailed Tanner in the head with a paddle by accident."

"Fuck!" Josh cringed. "How bad is he?"

"I don't know. The medics took him away pretty quick."

Josh was frantic. There was no way he could stay there. He had to go.

"Josh?"

"Nathan, I have to go see him."

"You can't! You have to stay on duty. Look at this crowd."

The pain in Josh's heart was killing him. "Oh God, oh God…"

"Josh," Nathan asked softly, "you guys are more than friends, aren't you?"

"No!" Josh cried, "I just care about him. Which hospital?"

"UCLA Medical, I think."

"You think?" Josh choked.

Nathan harkened to something down the beach. "Shit. Someone's signaling for help."

Josh wanted to scream in frustration as Nathan urged him to rush to where Destiny was holding up her rescue buoy, alerting them to an emergency.

Nathan grabbed a rescue can and started to run toward her. He spun around and shouted, "Josh! Come on!"

About to explode from the worry, Josh tightened his grip on the can and raced after him.

※

It was madness. Josh sprinted from one trauma to another, and by the end of the evening, his relief came. Josh was beyond exhausted.

Josh had no solid information about Tanner and it seemed the more he asked, the more his co-workers scowled at him. Geez. Couldn't a guy care about his friend?

The moment he was set free, Josh ran to his car. Someone had taken Tanner's backpack from the hut. He had no idea who. He assumed it was a medic or another lifeguard.

Josh tried not to crash into anyone as he left the parking lot. He raced to UCLA Medical, his heart beating in his throat. He parked in a handicapped zone and sprinted to the ER, gasping for breath as he came up to an information desk. "I'm looking for Tanner Cameron, a lifeguard that was taken here for an injury."

"One moment, please."

The nurse didn't seem as eager to help as Josh wanted her to be. "Is he here?"

She looked up at a board on the wall with marker pen scrawled all over it. "No. There's no one here by that name."

"Are you sure?" Josh was dying.

"Yes."

"Was he here? Was he here and checked out?"

"Look, it's very busy. Could you have a seat?"

"No!" Josh was about to go room to room.

"If you don't calm down, I'll have to get security."
"Fine. Look. You said he's not here, right?"
"Yes. That's what I said."

Josh sprinted back out of the building to his car. He sat behind the wheel, found his mobile phone and dialed. His hands were shaking from exhaustion and stress. "Answer, Tanner, answer." It clicked to his voicemail. Josh dialed Tanner's home phone. Tanner answered. Josh almost fainted with relief. "Tanner!"

"Josh. Did you get my message?"
"No. What happened? Are you all right?"
"Yes. I'm home. They released me a few hours ago."

"Shit! I'm on my way." Josh dropped the phone onto the passenger's seat and sped out of the lot.

※※

Tanner held a bag of ice to his cheek. He stood at the bathroom mirror and lowered it, inspecting the bright redness of his skin. He touched the swollen area and winced at the pain, placing the icepack back on his face. He shut the bathroom light off and scuffed tiredly to the kitchen. Popping out a pill from a vial, he placed a painkiller on his tongue, swallowing it down with a mouthful of bottled water. His doorbell rang, followed by heavy pounding on the door.

Tanner set the icepack on top of a newspaper on the coffee table and answered it. It flew open the moment he unlocked it.

Josh appeared completely out of his mind. "Tanner!"
"I'm okay." Tanner stepped back as Josh entered the house.

As Josh gazed at him in agony, he touched his jaw and stared at his cheek. "What happened? I was worried sick."

"Come in. Sit down." Tanner closed the door.
"No. You sit down."

Tanner was led back to the sofa. Josh picked up the icepack and handed it to Tanner.

"I'm a little woozy from the painkillers." Tanner pressed the ice to his cheek.

Josh covered his face for a moment, then he dropped his hands to his lap and asked, "Tell me what happened."

"I noticed a kayak overturn in deep water. I called for an IRB and we attempted to contact the guy."

The concern Josh was showing touched Tanner deeply.

"We managed to get him flipped over but he didn't even realize we were there. He slammed me right in the face with the paddle."

"Fuck!" Josh fidgeted where he sat.

"It didn't knock me out, but Christ, I thought he'd broken my cheekbone."
"Did he?"
"No. I'm just bruised. They took me to the hospital to make sure."

Josh rose off the couch and paced, clenching his fists and running his hand through his hair.

"Josh?"

"I was going insane. The beach was a madhouse. All I wanted was for someone to tell me you were okay and no one could. Tanner, there has to be a way to let everyone know when something like that happens."

"I thought Nathan knew." Tanner removed the ice pack again. It felt too cold on his skin. He set it down and touched his face lightly. "Didn't he tell you?"

"All Nat said was you were hit by a paddle and brought to the ER."

Tanner shrugged. "That was it."

"How did you get home? I could swear your jeep was still in the lot."

"I caught a lift from Hunter."

"Was it him and Blake that took you to the hospital?"

"Yes. Jealous?" Tanner smiled. It made his cheek hurt but he needed to lighten Josh's mood.

Josh exhaled a long breath and plopped down on the coffee table in front of him. "Tell me what you need. Can I get you something to eat?"

"I should eat. These pills are making me high as a kite."

"What are you in the mood for?" Josh cupped his face gently, smoothing a thumb over his cold, sore skin.

"I don't know. I need to look at what I have in the kitchen."

"No. Sit still. Let me."

"You don't have to do this, Josh," Tanner said as he stood to go to the kitchen.

"Shut up and don't move." Tanner sat back down on the sofa at Josh's gentle urging.

Smiling at him in delight, Tanner had no expectations of Josh helping him out. He figured Josh would wait patiently at home while Tanner convalesced. This care was a bonus he hadn't anticipated.

"You have pasta and a jar of tomato sauce. Can I whip that up?"

"You don't have to."

"Where are you going?" Josh scolded. "Sit your ass back down!" He approached the couch, nudged Tanner to lie on it, raised his feet on top of a cushion and handed him the ice pack. "Stay."

"Yes, Nurse Elliot." Tanner smiled dreamily at him.

"If I have to tell you again, there'll be trouble."

Nestling back against the cushions, Tanner watched Josh prepare his dinner knowing he had a silly drug-induced grin on his face. "I love you, you know that?" he whispered softly, too soft for Josh to hear.

Tanner began dozing. He opened his eyes to see Josh bringing over a plate.

Josh placed Tanner's food on the low table and helped Tanner reposition on the sofa, handing Tanner the dish and a fork.

"Wow. It smells good." Tanner sniffed at the steaming meal. He twirled some spaghetti on his fork and tasted it. "This is the sauce from the jar?"

"I added some things to it." Josh returned to the kitchen bringing Tanner back a glass of orange juice on ice.

Tanner gobbled the pasta down hungrily. "What the hell did you add to it?"

"It's a secret."

Tanner didn't move as Josh dabbed his chin with a napkin.

"You cook?" he asked, touching it after Josh had walked away.

"A little."

"Wow." He ate another bite. "Even Anna couldn't cook like this."

"Sorry?" Josh shouted, as he kept busy in the kitchen.

"Nothing." Tanner devoured the meal enthusiastically. Josh set a plate of garlic bread in front of him. Tanner asked, "Did I have that in the house as well?"

"You had the bread."

"Christ, it smells great." Tanner pulled a section off the roll and dabbed up his sauce. "Are you joining me?"

"Yup."

Watching Josh get his own dish and come back to eat with him, Tanner chewed the garlic bread and moaned in delight. "You made this?"

"You know they say the way to a man's heart is through his stomach. Any truth to that rumor?"

"Hell, yeah." Tanner shoved the chunk of bread into his mouth. "Anna couldn't boil water."

"Really? Did you always order out?"

"Pretty much."

"I have to admit I don't cook for myself very often. I did while Luis and I were together."

"He's an idiot." Tanner mopped up the rest of his sauce with another crusty slice of bread. He caught Josh's modest smile and grinned back.

Tanner welcomed Josh to cuddle next to him on the couch after the dishes were washed and dried. Josh was even nice enough to give him control of the television remote. Tanner took it, clicking on the television. Once they found some sports to enjoy, Josh urged Tanner to his lap on top of a pillow.

Feeling drowsy from the pills, Tanner snuggled in as Josh ran his hand through his hair, massaging his scalp.

His eyes falling to half-mast, Tanner couldn't remember feeling this safe and nurtured. Yes, he and Josh shared some physical pleasure, but this?

This was on a different level entirely.

Having fallen asleep on his lap, Tanner was woken by Josh whispering his name.

"Let's get you to bed, Tanner."

Hazy from the medicine, Tanner sat up, feeling disoriented. Josh helped him to his feet and brought him to the bathroom.

There, Tanner brushed his teeth, washed his face, and relieved himself. Once he was done, Josh escorted him to the bedroom, taking Tanner's clothes off and tucking him into bed. Josh placed Tanner's pills and a glass of water next to him on the nightstand.

"Goodnight, Tanner." Josh kissed his forehead.

"Where are you going?"

"Home."

"Why?"

"Why?"

"Set the alarm. Come to bed."

"Is that the Vicodin talking?"

"Who cares? No. It's me talking."

Josh left the room for a minute. Tanner could hear the water running in the bathroom. Stretching lazily, Tanner set the clock radio before he rolled over to watch the hallway for Josh's return.

Tanner felt the bed shift beside him and a warm naked body wrapped around him. Moaning in pleasure, Tanner squeezed Josh tight and fell asleep.

# Chapter Twelve

The alarm buzzed. Tanner whacked it to shut up. After a ten minute snooze, it went off again. Tanner shut it off and rubbed his face tiredly, touching the soreness of his cheek.

Tanner just remembered Josh had spent the night. "Morning."

Josh stared at him. "Morning."

"How bad do I look?" Tanner asked.

"It's getting a lovely purple color to it right under your eye."

"Nice."

"Makes you look rugged." Josh kissed him lightly. "You're not going to work looking like that, are you?"

Tanner frowned. "Yes. Why?"

"Do you think you should? You can't take the pain killers."

"I'll be fine." Tanner felt slightly embarrassed when Josh assisted him in standing up. "I'm okay, Josh. Really."

"Let me baby you. I'll make the coffee."

Tanner stared at Josh's bare ass as he left the room "You're spoiling me." He heard Josh's laughter. "Christ, I could get used to this." Tanner inspected his reflection. "Nice. Real nice," he muttered sarcastically.

When Josh returned he asked, "How do you feel?"

"It's sore but not unbearable." Tanner splashed his face.

"Take a damn day off."

"What? And be without you? Are you kidding me?"

The look on Josh's face was adorable. He appeared genuinely surprised. "You mean that?"

"I do." Tanner kissed his slack mouth. "Want to borrow a razor?"

"I don't know. I might cut myself. I'm in a state of shock."

"Here." Tanner located a new blade for him and the shaving gel and glanced over at Josh. Tanner noticed all the excitement had gotten to Josh. Josh's cock was standing at attention. "Did I say the magic word?" Tanner chuckled.

"Just looking at you, Tanner. That's magic enough." Josh leaned against the doorframe.

Tanner crouched down and kissed the tip of Josh's cock, then backed up to continue preparing to shave.

"Are you still high on pain killers?"

"No. I don't think so. Maybe the conk on the head knocked some sense into me." Tanner coated his face in shaving foam.

"Did it?" Josh's movie star smile appeared.

"I think I should know a good thing when it hits me in the face. What do you think, Josh?"

"Even when it's a male thing?"

Tanner shrugged and ran the razor over his jaw.

"What did I do to change your mind?"

Tanner glided the blade over his top lip, rinsing the razor in the basin. "I don't know. Maybe you're just the best thing that's ever happened to me."

"Hang on…back up…my head is spinning," Josh said, reaching out to brace himself on the doorframe.

Smiling at him adoringly, Tanner leaned closer and kissed him, leaving a trail of foam on his face.

"Please don't play a game like this, Tanner. You know how I feel about you."

"I do." Tanner continued to shave. "And I know even more after last night."

"What did I do last night?"

Tanner stood tall and gazed at him. "You act like you don't know."

"Know what? What am I supposed to know?"

"You showed me how much you care about me."

"Didn't you already know that?"

"Maybe not. Maybe sometimes it takes something more than a great blowjob." Tanner finished shaving. He could feel Josh's eyes on him as he rinsed his face in the sink.

"What could be better than a great blowjob?" he teased.

"Realizing someone loves you." Tanner caressed Josh's hair. It was as if he'd had an epiphany overnight. This was a man who cared deeply for him. It was an amazing feeling. In reality, Tanner knew he felt the same. Look at this man. Would there ever be another Josh Elliot? No, not in his lifetime there wouldn't be. And he'd be crazy not to recognize Josh's many virtues.

"I do, Tanner. I do love you."

Feeling his chest warm with pleasure, Tanner smoothed his hand down Josh's satiny side. "Yes. I finally got that message, Josh."

"Took you long enough." he chuckled.

Tanner patted Josh's bottom affectionately and reached into the shower and turned on the water. He stepped into the tub and wet down. Josh joined him. "Hello." Tanner felt his body react to the surprise.

"You mind?" Josh asked appearing bashful.

"No. I don't." Tanner shampooed his hair while Josh lathered up Tanner's cock.

"Should I stop? Do you feel up to it?" Josh asked, his fingers pausing as they held Tanner's shaft and balls gently.

"No. Don't stop. I feel fine." *Suck my balls please.* Tanner smiled in delight.

Tanner rinsed his hair, as Josh made sure Tanner's genitals were soap-free before he dropped to his knees.

Tanner couldn't wait to feel his mouth on him again. "Oh yes!"

Holding the wall and shower door, Tanner gazed down at that soaking wet beauty toying with the tip of his dick, brushing it against his tongue, working him at a fast pace. Tanner knew they didn't have all morning to lavish in passionate play. Chills washed up his spine and the water cascaded down his back, Tanner thrust his hips into Josh's mouth.

"That's it..." he moaned in delight as the sensations came to a head. When Josh pushed his wet finger up his ass, Tanner spun with the climax, shuddering down to his toes. His cock was completely enveloped by Josh's mouth and throat. Once he'd come, Tanner opened his eyes to see Josh's mischievous grin.

"You gorgeous hottie. Come here."

Josh hopped to his feet and wrapped around Tanner for a hug and kiss. Tanner spun them around so Josh could shampoo his hair under the spray. While Josh was occupied, Tanner squeezed watermelon-scented soap into his palm. Once he had lathered Josh's genitals up, Tanner ran his hands fist over fist along Josh's cock, making him shiver and pause in his scrubbing.

"Nice?" Tanner loved it. Just seeing Josh's reaction was worth everything he owned.

"Tanner..." Josh reached for his arm, bracing himself.

Eying Josh's seductive posture, his hips thrust forward, his head back, his eyes sealed shut. Tanner licked his lips in anticipation as Josh squeezed his arm tighter.

"Come. Come you sweet man. I want to feel your cum." Tanner couldn't believe it was his voice saying those naughty words. Never had Anna allowed him to talk dirty.

Tanner felt Josh's cock quiver and soon Josh grunted in pleasure. Josh thrust out his hips and ejaculated, sending creamy spatters onto his skin. "That's it, baby."

Josh opened his eyes and fell against Tanner, hugging him. "I love you so much."

Tanner kissed his cheek in thanks. "Rinse. Let's get a cup of coffee and go. It's getting late."

Smiling adoringly at him, Josh washed the soap off his bronze body and dark hair quickly.

Josh held his own backpack, watching Tanner shut off lights and the coffee pot. Before they sprinted out the door, Josh stopped Tanner and held him still. "You sure you're up to it? It was a zoo yesterday. And Saturdays are worse than Fridays."

"I'm fine."

Josh whispered, "Last kiss before work?" Josh was swung into Tanner's arms and dipped like it was a scene from some romantic movie. Josh, back on his feet, gaped at him. "Holy shit."

"Will that hold you?" Tanner laughed, locking the house up behind him.

"Hell, yeah."

"Good. Let's go."

While Josh drove them to the beach, Tanner found his hand and held it. Josh was so shocked at Tanner's change in attitude, he was almost more afraid. It seemed too good to be true and Josh knew better than most that fairytales rarely have a happy ending in real life. He kept waiting for the other shoe to drop.

Josh pulled into the lot and Tanner quickly released his hand. At the obvious gesture of separation, Josh felt his mouth form a tight line. So close but still so very far away.

Before Josh could even close his convertible roof, Tanner jumped out of his car as if he were petrified someone would see them come in together and surmise they had spent the night in each other's company. Josh's warm countenance faded. *Used again. What a surprise.*

Josh tried not to feel too hurt. But he kept asking himself, what did it take? What did it take for one man to come out and declare their love for another man? A miracle? What?

Josh waited as Tanner took a quick look at his jeep and nodded to Josh, meeting him by the cement steps.

Josh stood by as Tanner was confronted by his supervisor and questioned about his injury.

Josh kept quiet, leaning against the wall, as they debated on Tanner's health and fitness for duty.

"Hey." Nathan entered the room. "Tanner's here?"

"Yeah."

"Why didn't he take the damn day off?"

Josh shrugged.

Chris and Noah entered the room.

"Hey, lovebirds," Chris teased Nathan and Josh.

"Shut up," Nathan growled. "He did it as a joke."

"Sure he did, Nat." Noah laughed at him.

Trying not to listen to the taunting, Josh gazed back at Tanner. No. Tanner would not want to be on the receiving end of that type of tormenting. No way.

"Whoa, what happened to Tanner's face?" Chris whispered.

"He got whacked with a kayak paddle," Nathan replied.

"Ouch! That must have sucked."

Tanner approached them.

"Right. Ready, Josh?"

The others walking in front of him to go to their own tower, Josh lagged behind to speak to Tanner. "The captain giving you a hard time?"

"A little. He wasn't sure the doctor was correct in letting me return to work."

"Really?"

"Never mind. I convinced him it looks worse than it is." Tanner carried his backpack over his shoulder, his eyes focused out in the distance.

As Josh walked along the soft sand with Tanner, Noah twisted back to them and teased, "Hey, Josh, you want to walk with loverboy?"

Tanner jolted.

Josh's anger rose at the comment but also Tanner's reaction. He wanted to shout, 'Don't worry, Tanner, he doesn't mean you!' But thought better of it.

"Shut up, Noah." Josh pushed him from behind.

Nathan appeared pale from the ribbing. Obviously being labeled gay wasn't anyone's idea of a joke.

Walking silently with Tanner, Josh could hear the other men snickering.

"What's going on?" Tanner asked, looking confused.

Chris and Noah denied any wrong doing. Nathan spilled the beans. "They keep teasing me and Josh, Tanner."

"Why?"

Josh could see the veins in Tanner's neck pulsate. *Take it easy, Tanner, you're not the one they're accusing of being queer.* Josh kicked at the dry sand as he walked on.

"Shut up, Nathan." Chris shoved him to stop him from talking about it.

"No, you shut up! I told you. Josh was making a joke."

Tanner rubbed his eyes tiredly. "Why do I feel like a kindergarten teacher?"

"Never mind, Tanner," Noah whined.

Tanner stopped the other men. "Hold on."

The three stooges halted, turning around.

"Is this still about that kiss?" Tanner asked.

"Yes!" Nathan complained. "And it was a stupid joke. I don't like Josh that way. I don't like any guy that way. I like Samantha." At the admission, Nathan turned beet red.

Josh couldn't bear the conversation. How delightful to learn that being with a man is nauseating? He had to withstand it constantly.

"Listen to me, you morons," Tanner warned. "First of all, there is nothing wrong with being gay."

Josh held his choking cough at the damn joke. It sounded like the other three couldn't as they made all sorts of sounds in disbelief.

"Shut up and let me finish." Tanner pointed a warning finger at them. "And second, if I hear any more on this topic, I will take disciplinary action. You got it?"

"Yes, Tanner," they echoed softly.

"Get lost." Tanner waved them off. As the men made their way farther down the beach, Tanner touched Josh lightly. "You all right?"

"I'll live."

"Ignore them. They act like a bunch of juvenile delinquents."

"You think so, Tanner?" Josh replied sarcastically. "I think your act rivals theirs." He climbed the ramp to the hut carrying his backpack with him.

⁂

Tanner staggered slightly at the rebuking. He trailed behind Josh to dump off his belongings in the hut, thinking about Josh's comment. He was not happy about it.

By mid-morning the crowds had once again materialized. The binoculars to his eyes, Tanner scanned the beach, the water, and the other towers to make sure no one was in distress.

Four young men had set up a net to play volleyball a few yards from them. Tanner noticed two of the men point Josh out to the others. Tanner found Josh staring at the sea, his shaggy mane of dark hair blowing in the stiff breeze, his skin glowing shiny and bronze, and his dark designer sunglasses on his nose.

The white ball began to get popped back and forth vigorously. Tanner regained his focus and watched for any sign of problems.

The volleyball rolled to the front of their hut. Tanner lowered the binoculars.

One of the fit young men hurried behind it. He stopped directly in front of Josh. "Hey."

"Hey." Josh smiled at him.

"Hot one today, huh?"

"It is."

While Tanner observed, the young man glanced his way quickly before jogging back to the other three to pitch the ball over the net again. Approaching Josh at the rail, Tanner leaned his elbows on it and brushed against him. "Looks like you have an admirer."

"Do I?" Josh tilted to look.

Tanner did as well. Two out of the four players were ogling Josh. Once Tanner turned his attention back to Josh, he found his gaze on the distant water. "I think being in lifeguard red is a turn-on for some people."

Josh laughed softly.

"You okay?" Tanner stroked Josh's back gently, but didn't linger on it.

"Yes. Fine."

He didn't seem fine. He seemed preoccupied. "Are we getting together after work?"

"If you want."

"If I want? Josh?"

"Tanner? Your turn." But Josh didn't smile as he usually did when they played that game.

"You're upset with me."

"A little."

"What did I do?" As Tanner spoke, he kept his attention on the crowd.

Josh didn't respond.

"Josh?"

"Tanner?"

"Cut it out." Tanner nudged him. "Answer me."

"Do you really want me to discuss our personal business here and now? What happened to your 'Oooh! Not at work!' credo?"

That took Tanner by surprise. He had thought after last night they had grown closer not drifted apart. "What am I missing here?"

A sad sigh preceded Josh's reply. "Let me patrol the beach." Josh reached for a buoy. "See you in a bit."

Watching Josh walk off, Tanner straightened his back and tried to analyze the situation. He was puzzled.

The minute Josh was nearby, the boys with the volleyball seemed to miss their shot deliberately and the ball rolled right to Josh's feet. As two of the young men circled their prey, Tanner felt very uncomfortable. Was it possible for a male couple to have a committed relationship? Did he want one of those with Josh?

Seeing the young men smiling and laughing with his lover, Tanner had no idea what to do. But one thing was certain. He was hotly jealous. Instantly he had the urge to rush over and declare his love for Josh, keeping the hounds at bay. But he didn't have it in him. Being alone with Josh to share their love together was one thing, but here? On the beach, in public, in front of his co-workers? He was not ready for that. Not by a long shot. Or was he?

⁂

"What time do you get off from work?" the blue-eyed blond asked Josh.

"Eight. Why?" Josh peeked back at the tower. Tanner's gaze was riveted on them.

"Come out for a beer." The brunette rubbed Josh's shoulder seductively.

"Can I think about it?" Josh noticed the two men on the opposite side of the net staring at him.

"Sure." The brunette's hand slid slowly down Josh's arm to his wrist, giving it a squeeze.

Josh waved at them, continuing to walk to the water's edge. He felt their eyes on him and tried not to lose focus on the job. Inhaling the sea air deeply, Josh pretended he was in an exclusive relationship with Tanner, but even after last night he wondered if he was. It was obvious Tanner was not ready to go public with their love. Josh tried to believe it was more because the job than out of Tanner's fear of commitment. But if they came out as a couple, there was nothing the brass could do about it. In the age of political correctness, a gay couple became bulletproof.

They weren't hiding in the hut, giving each other head. They were purely professional on duty. No one could fault their dedication. No. This was Tanner's terror at the label. Josh was convinced.

Thinking of his three horrible relationships, Josh got a gut feeling this tryst with Tanner was going to end up the most painful. At least the men playing volleyball were gay. It made a difference. They were past the fear and the hiding. Josh could easily imagine holding hands with the pretty brunette as they strolled along the sandy beach. Maybe they would kiss as they sat together at dinner.

Tanner would never be able to do that. Though Josh didn't want to admit it, it would eventually drive him crazy to constantly pretend he was straight. "Been there, done that. And I won't do it again."

His feet splashing through the foamy tide, Josh paused to gaze out at the bobbing bathers and distant surfers. He took a good look at the towers on either side of theirs to make sure no one was signaling for help before he continued on his patrol.

Was he crazy to think a straight man would make him happy at home? And even crazier to fall for Tanner? Each time Josh said the three magic words, Tanner never returned the sentiment. "Christ, take the hint." Josh shook his head in disappointment at his own stupidity.

*Whose fault is it, Josh? I offered to suck him off. So? I've got no one but myself to blame if I'm being used for sex again.*

A young woman in a string bikini brushed up against his arm. "Hey."

"Hello." Josh didn't smile. He was in no mood.

"My friend needs mouth-to-mouth resuscitation." She giggled and pointed back to another young girl blushing brightly from humiliation as two other girls held her from escaping.

"She looks fine to me."

"What's your name?"

"Josh. Look, I have to keep moving."

"Okay. See ya around, Josh!"

Brooding, Josh continued walking down the beach.

༺༻

Tanner kept his attention split between the growing mob of people and his lover. The binoculars to his eyes, Tanner watched as a woman approached Josh, only to see Josh continue on his way. "Another admirer, Mr. Elliot?" Tanner glanced over at the four men still smashing the volleyball over the net aggressively. He wondered what they said to Josh. "Probably asked you out." Tanner bit his lip. "You're too handsome to be a lifeguard, Joshua. You'll get come-ons nonstop this summer." And the fear that Josh would be tempted haunted Tanner.

Tanner remembered Anna's jealousy well. How many times after her workday or during the weekends while he was on shift, did she sit beside his tower, watching every contact he made with suspicion? He wished she had been there to keep him company, to spend time with him. But he knew better than that. In the end it was a distraction he couldn't deal with. Each time a woman approached him for even a simple question, Anna scowled and the interrogation would hit the minute he began walking back to section headquarters for the night. That didn't even count the way she felt about his female co-workers. It made Anna an insecure wreck.

Was he feeling that way with Josh? What would he do if Josh met one of those handsome, fit young men for a drink after work?

He'd go completely insane with jealousy. Tanner could visualize his rage and the screaming match.

"Whoa." Tanner chided himself for that reality. "What the fuck am I supposed to do to stop him? Buy him a ring?"

When it came to gay protocol, Tanner was lost. He didn't know how to play that game, had no idea of the rules, and certainly couldn't question anyone about it.

Imagining asking Josh to be exclusive, to not going out with anyone else, Tanner felt goose bumps rise on his arms. What would that mean if he did? What would that make him?

"Gay." Tanner frowned, glancing back at the four fit men who took a break from hitting the ball and swaggered like gamecocks to the water.

❦

Josh was almost at the next tower down the beach, so he stopped to turn back. At a wolf whistle, Josh peeked over his shoulder. Noah was jogging toward him.

Noah collided with him, knocking Josh backward. "What are you doing in my neck of the woods?"

"Walking." Josh didn't smile.

"Mind if I join you for a little stroll?"

"I'm surprised you want to be seen with an out gay man." Josh switched the rescue can to his other hand so his and Noah's can didn't smack into each other.

Noah grinned demonically at him. "You like men's cocks?"

"Is that 'in general' or 'in particular'?" Josh was not happy with the conversation. He'd seen that smirk on Tom Ryder's face, just before he got shoved down onto a grassy field.

"Is there a difference?"

"Yes. A big one."

"I've got a big one."

"What's it got to do with me?"

Noah shrugged, still giving Josh a wicked grin. "If you like cock, I'll be happy to fuck you."

"Oh? Are you gay?" Josh wasn't amused and becoming more annoyed by the moment.

"Gay? Fuck no."

"You just offered to screw a man and you're not gay? Maybe you should re-evaluate your sexuality."

Noah stopped Josh's progress, holding Josh's arm.

Josh looked down at it impatiently.

"I'm just in between girlfriends and I need to get off."

"Again, I'll ask the same thing. What does it have to do with me?"

"I thought all you gay guys were cock hungry. Man, I imagined you'd be chompin' at the bit to get nailed by a straight guy." His hold on Josh's arm tightened. "I know you want Tanner, but he's never going to give it to you."

Josh stiffened his posture and tilted his face away as Noah's fingers dug into his arm painfully.

"So stop playing your little fairy games and tell me when and where."

"Let go of me." Josh shrugged off his hold and continued his walk.

"I'll find you. You fags pretend you don't want it. But you all do."

Josh tried to put distance between them. Praying he wasn't being followed, Josh felt icy cold in the hot breeze.

*That's what I get for coming out. Perfect. And thank you, Tanner, for making sure no one is aware we are a couple.*

He knew damn well if Tanner allowed that information to go public, Noah would never have dared to contact him that way.

Even from way off, Josh spotted the distress signal. Breaking into a run, he tried to close the enormous gap between himself and the tower beyond the one he and Tanner manned.

As he drew closer, he could see Tanner had grabbed his first aid pack and a can before he sprinted off. There was no way Josh could catch up to him. The distance was too great, and Tanner's speed was impossible to compete with.

A few hundred yards ahead of him, Josh finally had visual contact with the rescue in progress. Destiny and Samantha were dragging someone out of the surf. Tanner had arrived and was kneeling down next to the victim.

A whelping siren grew louder and Josh could see the rig advancing between slow moving gawkers.

Once he caught up, Josh began shouting to get the crowd out of the way, clearing the path for the truck.

He didn't recognize the two medics that manned the emergency vehicle. They flew out of the truck and knelt next to Tanner.

Destiny stood, looked around first, then shouted at Josh, "We got it. Go back to your tower."

Though it was the correct call, Josh heard a slightly sarcastic tone to her order. Taking a last glance at Tanner from behind, knowing he must be feeling weary from his ordeal yesterday, Josh had the impulse to stay behind and walk him to their tower. Seeing Destiny's glare aimed his way, Josh gave up, pivoted on his heels, and walked back to his area of the beach.

"Christ, why does everyone hate me?" he muttered, swinging the can up and back as he walked.

༺༻

Once the victim was loaded on the rescue truck and on his way to the hospital, Tanner shouldered his paramedic backpack and picked up the rescue buoy.

"Thanks, Tanner."

"No problem, Destiny." Tanner made his way back to his tower.

As he drew closer, he found Josh leaning on the rail, waiting for him, eating a peach from their lunch.

"The guy okay?"

"Yeah." Tanner passed him, entering the hut and dropping his backpack down. Tanner spun around, Josh was staring at him from the doorway, still chewing on the pit.

"I'm starved."

"Have a sandwich." Tanner made a log entry on their paperwork.

"You want one?"

"Sure." Tanner finished writing before he turned around to face Josh. Thanking him for a sandwich, Tanner said, "We need to eat it outside where we can keep an eye on things."

Once they were both munching their lunch, Tanner leaned against the rail beside him and asked, "What happened earlier with Noah?"

"Nothing." Josh stuffed the last bite into his mouth.

"It didn't look that way from here."

Josh gave him a tired glance, brushing the crumbs from his hands.

"What did he say to you, Josh?" Tanner didn't think it was going to be a struggle to get an answer.

Josh swallowed his food and crossed his arms over his chest. "Look, Tanner, though everyone pretends that working with a gay guy is cool, nifty, and very politically correct, deep down, everyone can't stand me."

Pausing from his chewing, Tanner gave Josh a look of disbelief. "What the hell did the guy say?"

"Nothing. Forget it."

"Josh, I warned both Noah and Chris to lay off you. If they said something insulting, I think you should make a formal complaint."

"Are you kidding me? The staff already can't stand the sight of me. If I make a complaint, someone will kick my ass."

"That's absurd." Tanner finished his food. "No one is going to harm you."

"Drop it, Tanner." Josh picked up the binoculars.

Feeling terrible for him, Tanner rubbed the nape of Josh's neck under his soft, brown hair lovingly.

"You're being watched."

Tanner looked to where Josh was indicating. The men were back at the volleyball net, staring their way.

"Be careful, Tanner," Josh admonished, "if you get a gay label you'll have to kill yourself."

Meeting Josh's glare instantly, Tanner replied, "What the hell is going on, Josh?" Tanner dropped his hand to his side.

"You tell me." Josh puffed up in a challenge.

"We can't talk about this now." Tanner turned away from the pain in Josh's eye.

Josh gave a snort and retorted, "Predictable."

"Maybe us working together wasn't a good idea." Tanner sighed tiredly.

"You're right. It wasn't."

Feeling anguish in the pit of his stomach, Tanner was surprised at how much the idea of not working with Josh upset him. There was nothing he could do to stop Josh from not wanting to be his partner.

❧

Tanner stepped out of section headquarters, expecting Josh to be waiting for him at the cement steps. Walking to the lot, not seeing his red convertible, Tanner leaned against his jeep and dialed Josh's mobile phone number. "Where are you?"

"On my way home."

"Didn't we have plans?" Tanner looked at the busy street and sidewalks as the business crowd was set free from their offices.

"Did we?"

"Josh, what's going on?" Tanner was hurt.

"Nothing. I'm bailing before this gets worse."

"Bailing?" Tanner rubbed his weary eyes. "I'm coming over."

"What for? Another blowjob?"

"What? What the hell does that mean?" Interrupting before Josh answered, Tanner added, "I don't want to have this conversation on the phone."

"Whatever."

The line disconnected, Tanner climbed into his jeep and started it up. Just as he was about to back out, he noticed Noah and Chris heading to their cars. Catching Noah's eye, Tanner curled his lip in reflex and wondered what the hell he had said to Josh. Somehow, he felt the event earlier in the day had an influence on Josh's mood.

He parked on the street behind Josh's apartment building. Jogging to the front entrance, Tanner buzzed his unit number hoping he'd be allowed in. The door clicked open.

Relieved, Tanner made for the stairs and ascended them quickly. He stood outside Josh's door and rapped it.

It took a few minutes but it finally cracked opened.

Pushing back the door, Tanner found Josh on the phone, walking back to the kitchen, already changed into a pair of jeans and a tank top.

Closing the door quietly, Tanner set his keys down on the counter and tried not to listen, but he damn well did.

"No. I don't have to explain anything to you, Luis."

Hearing that name, Tanner bristled in anger.

"I have to go. Someone is here." Tanner grimaced as Josh's green eyes flashed toward him.

*'Someone'? I don't even rate as a friend?*

"Goodbye, Luis." Josh turned the phone off and dropped it to the kitchen table, moving back to the dinner he was preparing at the stove.

Tanner began to feel like an intruder instead of a partner. "What did I do, Josh?"

Josh slammed down a wooden spoon he was using. "You're not gay," Josh said in irritation. "I have to ask myself why I'm pursuing a man who has no intention of proclaiming to the world I'm his. Sorry, Tanner. I need that. I didn't realize how much."

It felt as if a knife blade was stabbing Tanner in the chest. "It's too soon."

"For you." Josh gave him his back and returned to tending his dinner.

Closing the gap between them, Tanner caressed Josh's hair. Josh stiffened at the touch.

"I wish you could see how hard this is, Josh." Tanner dug his fingers through the thickness of Josh's long locks. "It's all so new to me."

Still keeping his back to him, Josh muttered, "I know. I'm finished having unreal expectations, Tanner. They are the death knell of a relationship."

"You realize it's only been a little over a week." Tanner smoothed his hand down Josh's back to his bottom. "You expected me to swap from women to men that quickly?"

"Yes, unfortunately. And I can see that it's not going to happen."

"You can't give me more time to get used to the idea?"

When Josh spun around, his hand wound up on Josh's crotch. Tanner didn't remove it.

"Look, Tanner, though I'm a little bit of a novelty act and a way for you to get off in between girlfriends, I know inevitably you won't be able to come out and be up front about our partnership."

Tanner didn't answer, wondering about the truth in the statement. He pressed his fingers against the denim zipper of Josh's tight jeans.

"Especially at work where it means the most to me."

"Why does it mean the most to you at work?"

"Because it's where I am getting the most grief. Do you think anyone would give me a hard time if they knew you were my boyfriend?"

"Who's giving you a hard time?" Tanner stopped stroking Josh's zipper flap and held his hand. "You need to make a complaint, Josh. That's very serious."

"No! Just go. You're not helping me at the moment."

Another searing pain blasted through Tanner's chest. "What do you want me to do?"

"Man, are you thick or what?"

"Come out? That's my only option?" Tanner backed up. "I either announce I'm gay and your boyfriend or we're through one week after we started this relationship? Are you listening to yourself?"

"I should have known better than to seduce a straight guy. It's my fault. They make it look so damn sexy in the stupid videos." Josh opened the refrigerator and took out a bottle of water, drinking it. "But the reality sucks."

"So, not only do you want us to stop seeing each other outside of work, you want us to stop working together as well. Do I have it right?" Tanner was so upset he didn't know how to handle it. He certainly wasn't ready to call it quits, not now. He was growing used to the idea of touching Josh and adored him more than he wanted to admit.

"Yes. Do you talk to the captain or do I?" Josh crossed his arms over his chest.

"I will. I'm the one who asked for you to be my partner. I'll tell him you're not happy with me." Tanner felt a lump form in his throat. Maybe he was insane to think this had a chance in hell.

"Fine. Tell him whatever you want. Maybe you should just tell him the fact that I'm a nasty queer is nauseating to you."

"Joshua!"

"Whatever. Let me eat my dinner before it gets cold."

Tanner didn't want to go. He had no idea he felt this strongly about Josh and would be heartbroken over parting.

"You still here?" Josh asked in irritation.

Turning away, Tanner picked up his keys and left Josh's apartment. Pausing once he was outside in the hall, Tanner felt his emotions well up and wondered how he had fallen so hard for Josh. He wasn't gay.

Or was he?

He clenched his teeth as he drove. Tanner was so furious he didn't know how to handle it. *One week? You give me one fucking week to get used to the idea of loving a man and that's it?*

"That's not fair." Tanner rubbed his wet eyes and winced as he pushed against the damaged tissue of his cheek. Finally pulling into his driveway, he climbed out, his backpack over his shoulder, and impaled the lock with his key. Storming through his living room, Tanner whipped the pack down violently and paced like a caged cat.

What the hell was going on? Why did this happen so quickly? Just yesterday he was lying on Josh's lap on the sofa getting pampered and being told he was loved.

"This isn't *fucking fair!*" He tightened his fist as he thought about Josh's ultimatum. "Come out? Tell my co-workers and supervisors I'm fucking gay?" Tanner thought that was a pretty tall order considering his history with women. His *long* history. "I've been straight for thirty years and gay for one week and I'm supposed to accept it and tell the world?" Tanner pulled back his arm as if to throw a punch at the wall. "How the hell am I supposed to do that, Josh!"

# Chapter Thirteen

Josh arrived at work the next morning, wondering if he was already reassigned. He had no idea how quickly a decision like that would be made.

Seeing Tanner's jeep, Josh felt a butterfly in his stomach. Trying to brave the day and whatever lay ahead, Josh entered headquarters and walked to the board. He was still assigned to Tanner's tower. Josh left the building to make his way down the beach checking the room for Tanner and seeing he wasn't there.

Before long he could see Tanner standing at the rail of the tower, gazing out at sea, his red windbreaker on protecting him from the chill of the morning air. It was overcast and black, flat-bottomed clouds loomed ominously over the horizon.

Stopping on the sand under where Tanner stood, Josh asked, "Did you request a transfer?"

"No."

"Why not?"

Shrugging, Tanner didn't meet his eye.

Josh walked up the ramp to drop off his lunch and backpack in the hut. How long were they supposed to play this game?

Josh stepped out finding Tanner was in the same spot, leaning his chin against his arms, which rested on the rail, his bottom was raised in a mildly erotic pose.

If it had been a day ago, Josh would have nestled his cock into that tight butt playfully to wriggle against him. Not today. He kept his distance.

"It's going to be dead today. They predict thundershowers."

Josh didn't answer. He scanned the beach. Not a soul was on it. A crackle of thunder echoed on the wind. The breeze picked up. Tanner walked inside the hut.

Out of curiosity, Josh peered in to see what he was doing. He was on the phone.

"Yes. Okay. No. It's fine."

Josh waited. Obviously Tanner was checking to see what he should do with the coming bad weather.

"Okay. Will do. Thanks." Tanner hung up.

Josh tilted his head in an obvious gesture.

"They want us to hang out in case it passes quickly."

Nodding, Josh walked back outside. Rain had begun pelting the sand and the ocean was choppy with whitecaps. Another white flash of lightning sizzled over the water. Right after, hearing the crack of thunder, Josh sought the safety of the contained hut.

With two hands, Josh hoisted himself to sit on the counter, swinging his feet lazily.

"Josh?"

"Tanner. Your turn."

A deep, soft laugh rumbled from Tanner's chest.

Josh watched him carefully, as Tanner approached. Suddenly they were alone with miles of wet and wild coastline surrounding them.

Tanner stood in front of him, pressing his body against Josh's knees. On reflex Josh sat back, away from him. Tanner nudged Josh's legs apart, making his way between them, gripping Josh's body to tug him close.

"What are you doing?" Josh asked, struggling not to get excited by Tanner's seduction.

"Thunderstorms scare me. Hold me."

Seeing the impish delight in Tanner's blue eyes, Josh let out a laugh. "Yeah, huh."

Josh melted when Tanner drew him to his chest, surrounding him with his embrace and pressing their crotches together. "Why are you doing this, Tanner?" he sighed, resting his chin on Tanner's shoulder.

A chill washed over Josh's body as Tanner nuzzled his neck, licking his skin and kissing his way to Josh's ear.

Another loud, hut-shaking thunder-crack blasted overhead. The heavy rain made a deafening racket on the roof and Plexiglas windows. The room grew dark as dusk.

Closing his eyes, Josh felt dizzy from the sweetness of Tanner's touch. Tanner's lips made contact with his and he groaned in agony as Tanner's tongue slipped inside. Josh's cock throbbed in his swimsuit against Tanner's, which was echoing the vibrations. Tanner cupped the back of Josh's head, sucking on his mouth passionately as the thunder growled and roared around them and the wind whistled through the window frames.

Josh opened his eyes when Tanner parted from his mouth. Tanner dug his fingers into Josh's hair, giving him a look of longing and adoration that made Josh's skin shiver with chills. Bright white flashed in a sequence like that of a strobe light, lighting the dark room, followed instantly by a sonic boom of noise.

It was so intense it made Josh flinch.

Hail began whipping against the walls and windows of the hut. It was deafening.

Tanner smoothed his hands over Josh's shoulders, down his arms and across his abs. When he came to Josh's swimsuit he began peeling back the waistband.

The storm was so loud Josh knew he'd have to shout to be heard, so he kept quiet. Josh held his breath as Tanner exposed his cock.

Josh choked in awe, seeing Tanner bend down to his lap. Josh felt a wave of dizziness wash over him the minute Tanner's mouth reached his cock, and wondered if it was some kind of hallucination brought on by the electrical storm.

"Oh, my God!" Josh shouted, but he couldn't even hear himself.

※※

All night Tanner had tossed and turned. And he knew one thing. He was not giving up on Josh. No way.

Through the wee hours of the morning, Tanner kept wondering on a way to make Josh see he could do this. He just needed some time.

Tanner could not lose a man as incredible as Josh Elliot. Tanner knew to win Josh back he had to take drastic measures. He had made a mental list of all those tactics as if he were drawing up battle plans. Transfer? No way. Break up? Not going to happen.

Suck him.

Show him you can do it. That you are not using him. Give it back.

That had to make a difference.

And in those early morning hours when no one should be awake, he imagined doing it. Taking Josh's cock into his mouth and sucking. He envisioned it so well he had jacked off to the thought. If it got him excited enough to come at three in the morning, he damn well was going to do it.

What a better opportunity than an isolated lifeguard shack in the middle of a thunderstorm? He couldn't have planned it any better. This was perfect.

Tanner never imagined chickening out. He was so anxious to try it, to please Josh, he decided to just do it. How bad could it be? If he couldn't tolerate it, then he'd make another decision. But until he tried it, he wouldn't be well informed.

He hated to admit Josh's scent, fresh from the shower, the feel of the smooth, spongy head in his mouth, was amazing. Tanner only wished he could hear his moans. It was so loud in the hut he couldn't hear his own thoughts. It only served to make the act surreal.

A salty drop coated his tongue. Could he swallow? Tanner didn't think he could, but for Josh he'd gag it down if he had to.

Tanner increased his sucking power, feeling Josh's fingers digging through his hair. He knew damn well what it felt like to get a good blowjob. An expert had showed him. Tanner was going a little mad himself, rubbing his rigid dick against Josh's shin.

"Tanner!"

*That* Tanner heard. Josh was warning him. He was ready. Tanner sucked harder, faster. Against his lips, Josh's cock vibrated simultaneously with another roaring blast of thunder. When cum shot into his mouth, he was stunned even though he had expected it. As it pooled on his tongue he closed his eyes and gulped it down before it choked him. He set back to see the results on Josh's face, giving his cock a last, lingering slurp.

He appeared stunned. That alone gave Tanner a reason to smile.

In the flickering light, Tanner was drawn to Josh's lips. The kiss was as electric as the storm outside.

Tanner gripped Josh so tightly he lifted him off the counter and onto his body. Josh clung to him, wrapping his arms and legs around his torso as he rocked back and forth, kissing him in ecstasy.

Parting to get a breath and see Josh's eyes, Tanner mouthed slowly, "I love you."

Everything he owned was worth the expression of astonishment on Josh's face.

Tanner buried his face into Josh's hair and closed his eyes, trying to feel strong and confident and not scared to death.

❧❧

Josh leaned close to the window to see the rain still coming down in sheets. Feeling warmth behind him, he wriggled against Tanner affectionately, reaching back to touch him.

Hungrily, Tanner kissed his hair and neck.

"Still not a soul around," he sighed, pressing his bottom against his crotch.

"A thunderstorm raging? I doubt too many people will show up at all today."

Josh smiled at his thoughts. "Wanna screw me?"

He felt Tanner jerk at the comment. "How?"

Tilting over his shoulder with an incredulous look, he echoed, "How?"

"No. I mean, don't we need a few things?"

"Hang on, handsome." He moved away from Tanner's embrace to his backpack, producing a rubber and a small tube of lube.

"You carry that with you?" Tanner exclaimed.

"Only since we've met." Josh moved closer. "Interested?"

"Wow. Anal sex? Am I ready for that?"

"Let's see…" He put on a thinking face. "I've sucked yours, you've sucked mine, you let me stick mine in yours…hm, I owe you one."

Tanner moved to the window and took a long look. Josh could see the area was desolate.

"What do I do?" Tanner gestured to himself.

"Let me handle it." Josh set the items on the counter. He reached into Tanner's swimsuit and found his semi-erection, working it hard in seconds. "What a cock you have, Tanner." Josh teased, as he exposed it.

"Thank you." He laughed.

Rolling the condom on, Josh lubed it up for him, and shimmied out of his own swimsuit. Stepping out of one leg, he held Tanner's hand as he walked to the window ledge. Once Josh had leaned forward, exposing his bottom, he said, "Go for it."

"That's it? Just push in?"

"That's it." Josh laughed at his surprise.

With his chin on his arm, he kept a lookout of the surroundings as Tanner pressed his cock against his back door.

"You okay?" Josh asked.

"I think so. I just can't believe I'm about to do this." Tanner sounded nervous.

"You don't have to if you don't want to." Disappointment washed over him.

"I want to. Believe me."

"Good." Josh tried to look over his shoulder. To help, he reached between his own legs and made sure Tanner was on target, then pushed back.

"Wow."

Josh smiled happily, squirming backward to meet his body, making sure he was all the way inside.

"Holy shit, that's tight."

"Mm…pump, big fella," he urged.

Holding his hips, Tanner began moving in a rhythm. "That's it," Josh crooned.

"Can I go faster?"

"You can do as you like."

"I don't want to hurt you."

"Are you kidding? It feels amazing, Tanner." He gave a good hard shove backward.

"Ah!"

"I'm not breakable." It was wonderful to be connected to him like this. In his wildest dreams he never imagined it would be this good.

Josh felt Tanner adjust his grip, using the tighter hold to thrust deep and hard.

"That's more like it," he crooned happily. "Yes! Fuck me! Fuck me hard, handsome!" Hearing an assortment of whimpering moans, Josh closed his eyes and centered all his concentration on their connection. Squeezing his muscles as tight as he could around Tanner's cock, Josh felt him thrust in sharply and heard his grunting over the pelting rain. Josh knew he was climaxing as Tanner's grasp on his body intensified. "Yes. That's it, baby…yes."

Tanner's weight collapsed on top of Josh's back. It felt like heaven to him. Raising his head, Josh noticed a truck coming down the wet sand toward them. "Tanner. Pull out. Someone's coming."

"Shit!" Tanner stumbled backward, yanking off the spent condom to wrap in paper towels. Josh was glad to see him jam it into the trash bag, all the way to the bottom.

As Josh dragged his suit up his legs, Tanner flipped his dick back into his swimsuit then used sterilizing cream on his hands, rubbing them together like a surgeon.

The truck stopped.

Tanner rushed to the door of the hut and opened it. The rain had lessened but not ceased completely. A fine spray was still misting the air.

"Captain," Tanner greeted him.

"Everything okay, Tanner?"

"Yes, sir."

"Good. After that thundershower I just wanted to make the rounds."

"Thank you, Captain."

"Sir." Josh nodded to the captain.

"Hello, Joshua. You both seem to have made it through the worst of it."

Josh exchanged glances with Tanner. The irony wasn't lost.

"Yes, sir." Josh smiled at the captain.

"Good. Let me continue on." He waved and climbed back into the truck, making his way to the next lifeguard tower.

Josh stood on the front of the tower, watching him leave wet tire tracks in the soaked sand.

"Cool."

"What?" Tanner put his arm around Josh.

"A rainbow."

Over the choppy water was a perfect arc in a spectrum of colors, brilliantly lit from a sliver of sunlight.

"It's beautiful," Josh sighed.

"It certainly is." Tanner winked at him.

⁂

Josh waited for Tanner at the cement steps. The entire day was a washout. Only a few brave surfers showed up in the late afternoon to ride the large, turbulent waves left by the storm.

His windbreaker on, his backpack over his shoulder, Josh killed time by pressing his foot down against his wet squishy flip-flops, watching the air bubble out of them. He looked up to see someone stood before him.

It was Noah. Josh rolled his eyes tiredly. Chris met up with them and Josh assumed Noah would be too embarrassed to torment him sexually in front of his macho friend. He was wrong.

"Waiting for me?" Noah asked, giving Chris a demonic grin.

"No. Get lost." He wondered what Chris would think of Noah's actions.

Chris leaned against his right side as Noah sandwiched him on his left.

"Stop it. Leave me alone." Josh shoved at each of them in turn, but they didn't move.

"You know you love it." Chris laughed.

"Says you. Get lost." He tried to shift away from them.

"All you gay men are sexaholics." Noah tugged on his hair.

Josh swatted his hand away. "Jesus, what is with you guys? Can't you take the hint? I'm not interested."

"Sure you're not." Noah grabbed his ass and squeezed it.

"Cut it out!" Josh pressed him back. Suddenly he was beginning to feel a sense of déjà vu. A memory of two football players pinning him against a locker in high school made him shiver.

"A gay man not interested in sucking a straight guy's dick?" Chris hissed, "Liar."

Twisting out of their grasp, Josh faced them in irritation. "No thanks!"

"Do it quick. In my car. Come on." Noah grabbed his hand and used it to stroke his cock.

Josh jerked his arm away. "Leave me alone." He started walking away. Instantly, both men had him between them again.

"If you touch my ass once more, I'm going to get violent." Josh ground his jaw.

"Why are you playing hard to get?" Noah teased. "I thought fags loved cock. Period."

"Get away from me!" Josh pushed them off simultaneously.

"What the hell is going on!" Tanner roared.

All three men spun around to see his fury.

Josh had a terrible feeling he was going to be blamed for this mess. He opened his mouth but nothing came out.

"Hey, Tanner." Noah appeared very casual, as if he had not just assaulted someone.

Josh gawked as Tanner grabbed Noah under the shirt collar and wrenched it into a knot, choking him. "What the fuck do you think you're doing to my man?"

He felt faint. Did he just hear right?

"Your man?" Noah gasped.

"Yeah. *My. Man.*" Tanner sneered, his lip curling.

"I...we...didn't know..." Noah stammered as Chris tried to disappear.

"Get over here!" He ordered Chris, shoving Noah back.

Josh stared at Tanner in shock.

Gripping one goon in each fist, Tanner drew them together so their heads knocked. "Listen to me, and listen good," he snarled. "If I find either of you have come near my lover again, I'll not only have you fired, I'll kick your ass. Understand?"

"Yes, Tanner!" they replied quickly.

"You want to file a complaint, Josh?" Tanner's glare never left the two men.

Josh shook his head, awed by the sight before him. "No. Just tell them to leave me alone."

"Did you hear or do I have to repeat it?" Tanner slammed them together again.

"We heard. Sorry, Josh." Noah looked pale.

With one last push, Tanner sent them stumbling away. As they left, looking back over their shoulders in amazement, Tanner hugged Josh.

"Wow. Am I dreaming or did you just do that?" Josh wrapped around him.

*~*

"You're not dreaming." Tanner set back from Josh. Seeing Destiny and Samantha coming up the cement stairs, he kissed Josh in front of them.

The flutter it sent through his mid-section made his knees weak. He must have lost his mind, but he was coming out, so he may as well make it all the way out.

"Holy shit!" Josh gasped as he parted from his mouth.

"Hello, ladies." Tanner smiled at them, his arm around Josh.

"We had a feeling," Samantha replied sweetly, while Destiny appeared pinched.

"Yeah. No point in hiding is there?" He kissed Josh's cheek.

"You lucky guy!" Samantha gushed.

"You got that right." Tanner grinned at him.

"So?" Destiny folded her arms over her chest. "You're gay?"

"Yup." He felt like he was high. "And? So?"

"And? So?" Destiny echoed, but her pout changed slowly to a smile. "You do make a cute couple."

"Thank you, Destiny." Tanner glanced down at Josh whose expression hadn't changed. Stunned seemed to be his permanent state.

"I'm happy for you guys." Samantha touched his arm.

"Thank you, Sam." He met Destiny's gaze.

"Me too, Tanner." Destiny finally gave in. "I think it's great."

"They think it's great, Josh." Tanner shook him playfully.

"Holy shit." Josh blinked and came back to life. "I can't believe you just did that."

"We have to go. See you, ladies." Tanner grinned at the women. "It's time for a little boy talk."

"Uh huh," Samantha replied, her tongue in her cheek.

He waved at them, leading Josh to his car. Once they were standing at the driver's door of the red convertible, Tanner straddled Josh's legs and connected their hips. "You okay?"

"I'm a little speechless."

"Those assholes won't mess with you anymore." Tanner pushed Josh's hair back from his forehead.

"No. I know they won't. They're scared of you."

He chuckled in reply. "Your place or mine for a little…" Tanner rubbed their crotches together, "man on man action."

Josh gave Tanner a smile. "You do love me?"

"I do."

"Wow."

"Wow," he mimicked.

"Want to go to my place for some pizza and porn?" Josh teased. Lowering his voice, Josh added, "You know…the gay kind."

Breaking up with laughter, he replied, "Sure, why not?"

"Yes!" Josh pumped his fist. "Follow me home."

"I'll follow you anywhere, Josh." He wrapped around him again for a kiss. It felt liberating.

"Wow!" Josh gulped, his eyes wide in awe.

"See you at home." Tanner parted from him, noticed some other lifeguards had seen, and suddenly, didn't care. What could be embarrassing about loving a man as amazing as Josh Elliot? He was proud to be his partner. Everyone else wished they were. He knew that.

Waving to Josh as he climbed into his car and left the parking lot, Tanner couldn't wait to begin a whole new life. Maybe this was just what he needed.

Josh was in heaven. He took a mental note of the date. June twentieth, the first day of summer, and the first day of the rest of his life. Seeing Tanner's jeep in his rear view mirror, he knew life just didn't get any better than this.

Smiling as the wind blew back his hair, Josh couldn't wait to get Tanner in his arms again. Just the two of them. Man to man.

# About the Author

G.A. Hauser was born in the shadow of the Manhattan skyline in the suburbs of New Jersey in the sleepy town of Fair Lawn. After graduating with a degree in Fine Arts from a university in New York, she gave up the idea of being a starving artist and headed for Seattle. For over a decade she lived in Rain City, and the last eight of those years she wore a blue police uniform working for the Seattle Police Department as a patrol officer. She's been writing since 1990 but it wasn't until she reached the wet British Isles that she published her first book, *In The Shadow of Alexander*. She lived in Hertfordshire, England for six years and from there she was able to travel and see the wonders of the world. She's back in the good ol' USA once again and is convinced *there's no place like home.*